GO DEEP

UNEXPECTED LOVERS: BOOK ONE

RILZY ADAMS

for Nikki.

CHAPTER ONE

Tired. Stale. Uninspired.

Navaya blinked and refocused her attention on her phone's screen but the words didn't change. Anybody who said words could do no harm probably never spent any time on book reviewing websites. They obviously never had to sift through almost sixty, one and two star reviews of something they poured themselves into. Reading reviews was always nerve-wracking for Navaya, so she generally stopped a few days after she put out a book. In those first few days, however, it was important for her to get a read of how people felt about her work. She groaned. The read she was getting was as clear as it was brutal. The people were *not* feeling her newest book, *Captive to My Desires.* In the six years Navaya had been writing, she'd never experienced such overwhelming negativity. And the book had barely been out for three days!

Tired. Stale. Uninspired.

She tried swallowing the lump in her throat, but her mouth was too dry. Navaya hated that tears pricked the corner of her eyes. Her skin should be thicker by now. There had been some *bad* reviews over the years. Hell, some of the reviews of *Captive to My Desires* were objectively worse than: *Tired. Stale. Uninspired.* The very first reviewer said they'd rather eat a pile of steaming dog shit than read anything else she wrote. That didn't sting, no... *burn*, as much as the three words emblazoned on her screen: *Tired. Stale. Uninspired.* She knew why they hurt so much. They gutted her because they were true. Navaya pinched the bridge of her nose, trying to ward off the panic that suffocated her. Her reviews had started becoming more critical over her last four releases and now she had to confront the fact that something was wrong. She wasn't hitting the spot anymore. Navaya knew she should stop reading reviews now she was drowning in her feelings, but apparently she had no sense of self-preservation. She scrolled down the page, wincing as she went along.

I remember when a Navi Howard release had me checking to make sure my vibrator had fresh batteries. I'm just bored now. Homegirl needs to focus on something else.

That review pushed Navaya from her office chair and straight to her kitchen. She shuffled through her cabinets until she found her largest wine glass and poured a generous serving of Cabernet Sauvignon before swallowing it in only a few gulps.

Tired. Stale. Uninspired.

The words mocked her as she refilled her glass and trekked to her living room where she curled up on her burgundy couch. Was she surprised her work was suffering, though? Navaya hadn't fucked anything that wasn't silicone or battery operated in nearly a year and a half since her no good ex, Callahan, put her off men. That was a pretty sorry state of affairs for somebody who made a living writing erotic fiction. Thinking about the son-of-a-bitch whose side chick found out she was pregnant after taking a pregnancy test in Navaya's bathroom and then left the stick on the counter for her to find had Navaya gulping the wine again. The last thing she needed to do when she was already low was think about that period of her life. Her grand-mother, Gertrude's, spirit had to have been with her. Callahan didn't get murdered and Navaya didn't get twenty to life. She'd flushed her engagement ring down the toilet, packed most of her shit up and left while he spluttered excuses that fell on deaf ears. She ran to the only person she trusted with her life; the only person who always knew how to make things better no matter how catastrophic they seemed. The same person she would run to now that the ramifications of how badly her latest release was flopping sank in. She glanced at her watch and cringed. It was pushing midnight. She hesitated for a while before she dialed her best friend's number. She hoped Xander wasn't balls deep in his girlfriend since the hour was so damn late. Navaya breathed a sigh of relief when he picked up after only two rings.

"Xander," she managed to get out before the tears she'd been holding back for the past forty-five minutes broke loose. "I know it's late but can you come over? I need you."

CHAPTER TWO

Can you come over? I need you.

The desperation lacing Navaya's voice made Xander's heart beat double time. What the fuck was going on? The last time Navaya called him crying like that, he nearly put a nigga six feet under.

"Hey Nav," he soothed. "What's wrong?"

She started talking about her newest book, bad reviews, Callahan ruining her life and a bunch of other things he could barely understand through her sobs.

"Don't worry, I'm coming," he said. He was already sitting up with his feet hung over the side of his bed as he disconnected the call. He was a little calmer now he knew she wasn't in any actual danger. He felt the bed shift and swallowed a groan. Xander was hoping he might have been able to sneak out and shoot Stefanie a text so she wouldn't be alarmed if she woke up and found him gone.

"You okay?" she asked, covering a yawn as she sat up in bed. The sheet dropped to her waist, offering him a full view of her perky, brown breasts. Xander sighed. He didn't need much time to put Stefanie back into an orgasm-induced coma, but he knew exactly what would happen once he told her where he was going.

"Nav needs help with something," he said. He waited for the fallout he knew was coming. Stefanie sat up straighter in the bed, her pretty face contorting into a scowl. "Now? It's nearly midnight. You act like you're her dog. She always expects you to come running whenever she calls."

Xander closed his eyes, took a deep breath and tried to let the irritation flow out of his body with his exhale. "She didn't *expect* me to come. She asked if I could, and I can."

"It's late," Stefanie said. Finality lined the edge to her voice. "You can help her with whatever she needs tomorrow."

Xander chuckled as he stood. "I wasn't asking for your permission to go, Stef. You wouldn't be tripping like this if Cole needed my help."

"If you leave, I won't be here when you get back."

Xander moved to the bathroom, washed his face and brushed his teeth. Stefanie stood next to the bed with her arms folded across her naked body when he returned to the bedroom. He grabbed sweats and a T-shirt before he turned to face her.

"Did you hear me, Alexander?" she asked.

"Quite clearly," he said. "Just lock the door behind you on your way out."

XANDER WAS STILL mad as hell as he made the drive from Silver Spring into Bethesda, where Navaya lived in a one-bedroom apartment in a complex right in the hustle and bustle of things. He hoped Stefanie followed through with her threat to leave. It would save him the effort of having to kick her out when he got back. She'd ended their relationship with that little ultimatum, whether she'd intended to or not. Xander wasn't too shaken up about it. He'd only been dating the pretty, caramel skinned barista, from the *Peet's Coffee* he frequented on his way to the Montgomery County middle school where he taught Science, for two months. Xander grimaced. He was going to have to find a new coffee shop now. He shook his head as he searched for a parking spot. *Another one bites the dust.* This was the fifth relationship to end because the woman was insecure about his friendship with Navaya. He was sick of it, but more than that, Xander was perplexed. He was always upfront about Navaya's presence in his life. They'd been best friends since they were literally in the womb. Navaya's mother, Kathleen, and his mother, Raquel, got pregnant within weeks of each other and they were determined for their kids to be the best of friends. They were disappointed when they realized they were having a girl and a boy, respectively, but that didn't deter them. Navaya and Xander were inseparable for their entire lives. His no good father walked out soon after he was born and Navaya's father, Franklyn, was one of the steadiest father figures he'd known until he succumbed to kidney failure when Xander and Navaya were fifteen. He and his mother lived down the street from the Howards and they joined them on every family vacation. He and Navaya attended the same pre-K, elementary school, middle school and high school. When it was time for University, nobody was surprised when they both chose to go to Howard University together. Navaya didn't think twice about staying in the DMV when Xander decided he would stay after graduation. Nobody could ever compete with that sort of history. And most of his partners seemed to accept that. Xander had always thought it was because as close as he and Navaya were, their boundaries were clear and they never disrespected the other's relationship. Cole used to clown the fuck out of him when he mentioned that was why Navaya and his last serious girlfriend, Megan, got along so well.

"You know you are a straight fool, right?" Cole had said. "Megan's only cool with Navaya because she's been dating Callahan for nearly seven years. She doesn't see her as competition. Remove that dick and watch all hell break loose."

He'd dismissed his friend's observation, but things really did start popping off once Navaya left Callahan's cheating ass a year and a half ago. He hadn't had one relationship last past four months since then and he was frustrated as hell. Xander was still ruminating over things as he entered Navaya's building with the fob she'd given him. He found her in her living room, curled up on the couch staring out the window. He couldn't see her face, but her sadness and frustration permeated the air around her.

"Nav?"

She flicked her gaze to him, wiped her face and got up from her couch. Navaya crossed the small distance between them and stepped into his open arms. He hugged her for a while, rubbing her lower back and tucking his chin into her box braids. Eventually she stepped out of his embrace and asked, "Remember my last book?"

He nodded, leading the way back to the kitchen where he grabbed a beer from the fridge and poured her another glass of wine. Navaya had been disappointed for weeks with the reception her last book received.

"Remember what I told you," he said. "Once it's out in the Universe, let it go and focus on the next one."

She laughed bitterly and shoved her tablet at him. "This one has gotten far worse reviews. I've gone from Navi Howard, erotic author extraordinaire, to worse than steaming dog shit."

He'd started telling her to stop exaggerating when his eyes

landed on the review that actually compared her writing to dog shit. Fuck. He wasn't sure what to say.

"The problem is that they are right," she whispered. "I've been uninspired. I've been celibate for so long I'm surprised I remember which body parts go into each other. Of course my writing seems stale."

Xander shuffled around Navaya's kitchen to the small jar she kept her marijuana and encouraged her to vent while he rolled them a joint. They settled back in her living room a few minutes later. He watched as she took a deep draw of the joint and held it for a while before she exhaled slowly. She passed it back to him and sipped on her wine. Navaya looked stressed as hell.

"It's an easy fix if your lack of a sex life is the issue."

She chuckled. "What? Should I put an ad on *Craigslist*? Celibate author of erotic fiction seeks inspiration?"

He laughed. Navaya was so damn dramatic when she wanted to be. "You could go that route, or you could just use *Tinder* like other normal people."

She rolled her eyes. "I have stranger danger, thank you very much. I'm not trying to end up as a feature on a show on *Investigation Discovery*."

Navaya took a deep drag from the joint before she smiled up at him, her brown eyes sparkling with mischief. "It's best I ask you to use your dick to mentor my pussy back to life instead of doing alladat. It'd be like a *mentordick* or something."

The beer Xander had been sipping went down the wrong way. He waited a few seconds after he recovered from his spluttering before he said, "Nah, Nav. You can't handle this dick. Tinder might have you on *Investigation Discovery,* but one hit of this and you'll be starring in your own episode of *Snapped*."

Navaya howled with laughter as she took the joint he offered her. "I hate you so much."

"You're right though. It's time to get both your creative and pussy juices flowing."

"You nasty as hell," she giggled.

Xander shrugged. "Nasty but right, Nav. Nasty, but right."

CHAPTER THREE

Navaya tried to pay attention to her breathing while she moved into *savasana* at the request of her yoga instructor. Hot Fusion Yoga was always an amazing way for Navaya to empty her mind, but her head was still crowded with the anxious thoughts that plagued her all through the night. The instructor walked around the heated studio passing out cool lavender towels. Navaya placed one on her forehead, hoping the lavender had the calming effect it was supposed to have. She needed it. Navaya was still replaying the reviews in her mind even as she headed to the bathroom to shower and quickly change for the early dinner she was having with her friend, Tasha, in forty-five minutes. The early fall weather was still pleasant, so she pulled on a fresh pair of black yoga pants and a lightweight pink sweater before shoving her feet into ballet flats. She pulled her box braids into a bun on top of her head, moisturized her skin with her favorite coconut body butter and swiped on a deep purple lipstick.

"Excellent class, Breanna," she said, waving at her instructor as she exited the locker room.

Breanna pulled her attention from the two clients she was checking in for the next class, "See you next week, Nav!"

Core Power was conveniently located a stroll up the street from her apartment complex but Navaya was sold when she'd walked into her first class and found that her instructor had smooth, chestnut skin; curly natural hair and a wide, open smile. Representation mattered far beyond books and movies.

Navaya burned time by strolling through the Target across the street and predictably picked up a few items she didn't need before she grabbed a chai tea latte from the in-store Starbucks and headed towards Woodmont Ave for her lunch date. She and Tasha chose the Mussel Bar and Grille because they rivaled each other in their absolute obsession for mussels. Xander often tolerated Navaya dragging him to the restaurant, but Navaya always felt guilty. Tasha was already sitting in one of the booths with two glasses of white wine when Navaya walked in.

"You've got the right idea," Navaya grinned, pulling the glass of wine to her and taking a sip.

"Well, you hit me with an SOS so I knew it was about to be serious," Tasha said tucking a bit of her burgundy-dyed natural curls behind her ear. "What's going on?"

Navaya went through the chaos that was the previous night down to Xander's stupid suggestion that she signed up to Tinder and her comeback that he should fuck her instead. Navaya loved that she and Xander had the kind of friendship where she could make those kinds of jokes without feeling like he'd take it seriously.

"Why does it have to be a joke?" Tasha asked just as the waitress put a sizzling plate of mussels in white wine sauce in front of her.

"How many glasses of wine did you have before I got here?" Navaya asked. "Cause you must be drunk."

"Oh, come on. Imagine your ass getting on Tinder looking

for a man to fuck some inspiration into you and then you go on your first hookup and the sex sucks. Then what? You start again and hope for the best?"

Navaya placed her elbows on the table, interlocked her fingers and brought her chin to rest on them as she gave Tasha the stankest look she could muster. "Thanks for making things worse, Tash."

Her friend brushed her off with a wave of her hand. "By contrast, we know Xander must be a good fuck from the way your roommate used to act all demon possessed whenever they had sex back at Howard."

Navaya made a face. "Let's not talk about that."

"I'm just saying, sis. You guys are solid. I can't see a little bit of sex ruining things between you but I can see that it might..." she paused as if thinking about her next words. "What did Xander say? Get your juices flowing?"

"I'm going to ignore you and eat now," Navaya said with a chuckle. She dug into her food, but Navaya couldn't put Tasha's ridiculous suggestion from her mind no matter how hard she tried. It started seeming more reasonable as she continued thinking about it. *Tired. Stale. Uninspired.* She winced, even now, when she thought of those three words. Maybe Tasha had a point after all. Navaya squeezed her eyes shut and took a deep drink of her wine. Yep. She was losing her goddamned mind.

CHAPTER FOUR

Nav: Will you be my *mentordick*?

Xander was in the middle of a poker game with his friends Cole, Jay and Quinn when the message came in from Navaya and shot his concentration to pieces. He sent back a few puzzled emojis and tried to keep his focus on the game while he waited for her to reply, but he was finding it hard. Cole ran his hand over his bald head as he took in his cards.

"You know everybody knows your tick, right?" Xander asked with a chuckle, happy to pay attention to something other than Navaya typing a response for what felt like the last ten minutes.

"Fuck you, man," Cole laughed. "Y'all know I hate poker."

Xander nodded, a wide grin spreading across his face. They all knew because Cole mentioned it every week. He'd met the dark, tall, muscular personal trainer a few years before when he joined a local gym trying to get ready for a marathon he never ended up running. They shared the same quick wit and love for music and became easy friends. Cole was the one who encouraged him to showcase his songwriting skills to the world and they formed a small band with Cole's younger cousin, Jay. Serenaded by Mahogany, or SBM as they called themselves, was one of the best decisions Xander had ever made.

"Why you looking at your phone like that?"

This was from Quinn, who taught Mathematics at the same school Xander worked.

"Look at you over there being light-skinned and nosy. It's not a good look."

Quinn rolled his hazel eyes. "Is it Stefanie?"

The question pulled Xander up short. He hadn't thought about Stefanie much since he returned home after comforting Navaya to find the drawer she kept at his place cleared out and a passive aggressive, well... *downright aggressive* note on his bed. He hadn't responded to the note or the several texts she sent afterwards.

"Stefanie's not on my mind," he admitted.

Jay laughed. "You're a frosty ass nigga. Who hurt you?"

Xander didn't pay him any mind. He wasn't frosty at all. Hell, Xander would say he was very good at relationships. He'd maintained civil contact with most of his exes and his last serious relationship only ended because Megan accepted a job in Japan and neither of them wanted to try a long distance relationship.

"Stefanie was tripping," Cole said. "You lucky she showed her ass before you developed any real feelings for her."

"But how many women is Navi going to cost you before you try to set her up with your boy so your little girlfriends can feel more secure?" Quinn asked.

"You know me and Nav stay out of each other's relationships, so you definitely on your own with that," Xander said with a little laugh. "I've been waiting for you to step to her so she can put your yellow skinned ass in your place."

"It be your own friends," Quinn shot back but his voice was

light. Xander's phone vibrated again. He checked the message, unable to stop himself from murmuring, "What the fuck?"

Nav: I need to get my juices flowing. Swing by so we can talk about available *mentordick* opportunities for this sex-starved pussy.

He looked up from his phone and found six pairs of varying shades of brown eyes looking at him with curiosity. Jay was the first to speak, "You good, man?"

He reread the message again. "I'm fine but I think Nav has gone and lost her mind. I'm going to have to head out."

"If you leave, we won't be here when you come back," Quinn said in his best imitation of Stefanie's voice.

Xander shook his head but laughed all the same. "Grow up."

He grabbed his phone, wallet and keys before draining his beer and heading out of Cole's house wondering what the hell was going on with his best friend.

CHAPTER FIVE

Damn Tasha for putting the thought in her head. Damn her mind for warming up to the idea. Damn the Cabernet Sauvignon for giving her the courage to see it through.

Navaya couldn't believe she'd just asked Xander to fuck her.

Xander. Her best friend for the entire thirty-one years she'd graced this earth.

Xander. The man who knew all her deepest, darkest secrets. *Shit.* What the hell had she been thinking? She was desperate, yes, but did desperation cause temporary insanity? Or, perhaps, permanent insanity? Because even though Navaya knew she should call Xander and tell him she was just playing around, she wasn't going to. The proposition was ridiculous. Yet, it made sense. There was no guarantee having sex would do a damn thing about her lack of inspiration, but if it *could* Xander was probably her best option. She trusted and was comfortable with him. And Xander was... hot. At six feet four inches, he had considerable height on her five feet seven inch frame. His dark, smooth skin contrasted nicely when he pulled his lips back and revealed bright, white teeth when he smiled. Some girl wrote him a love letter when they were in high school saying the waves in his hair made her seasick. Sis was corny as hell, but not inaccurate. Navaya just wasn't sure she could convince him that where her options stood he was really the best one. She was sitting around her dining room table nursing a glass of wine when she heard her front door open. Anxiety settled in Navaya's stomach even though she knew it was stupid to be nervous about Xander's reaction. Worst-case scenario was that he didn't agree with her, but even then the most she'd have to look forward to was a few days of teasing. He stood at the entrance to the dining room dressed in navy blue sweats and a white T-shirt, looking at her with curiosity sparkling in his eyes. Navaya tried to find the words to start the conversation but Xander spoke first.

"Mentordick?" His thick, full lips curved into a smirk. "What's going on with you, Nav?"

She gestured for him to join her around the circular, glass dining room table. "I'm being proactive."

"With *me*?"

His voice was filled with such astonishment that Navaya started to feel genuine regret for opening up Pandora's box. She knew what she was asking for was unorthodox, but was it *that* hard to believe that two persons comfortable with each other and in their relative sexual primes could hook up?

"Why do you sound like I'm asking you to turn water into wine?"

Xander massaged the back of his neck and held Navaya's gaze. His eyes were puddles of chocolate and incredulity. "I just can't believe you're not messing around."

"Why would I be?" she asked. She took a sip of her wine and started going over the list of pros she'd written down when she was trying to weigh her options earlier that afternoon. It took the guesswork out of Tinder. She trusted him. And, with the publication date for her next novella just about three months away, time was of the essence.

"What? You got cold feet after all the bragging you've done about your dick?"

Xander made a face. "That ain't nothing but the gospel truth. You've just forgotten the most important consideration."

Navaya ran back through her list in her mind but couldn't figure out what Xander was talking about.

"What?"

"Chemistry. Attraction. All of that has to be present for sex to be good. It doesn't matter how great my stroke game is."

It took a few seconds for his implication to sink in and Navaya felt her cheeks go hot. Embarrassment rushed over her in such a vicious wave that she almost lost her breath.

"Forget I asked," she mumbled. She pushed her chair back and started toward the kitchen, desperate to put some space between her and Xander. She'd barely made it into the kitchen before Xander was behind her. He grabbed her waist. "You all up in your feelings now, aren't you?"

There was amusement in his tone and that just made Navaya want to knee him in his groin.

"You just called me unattractive," she muttered. "Who wouldn't feel a type of way?"

Xander cocked his head to the side, set his lips into a straight line and raised his left eyebrow. It was his trademark reaction whenever he thought she was being over the top. It riled Navaya up even more. She started pulling out of his embrace, but he held her tighter. "Navi-Nav. I know you didn't hear those words come out my mouth."

"Chemistry. Attraction. All of that has to be present for sex to be good. It doesn't matter how great my stroke game is," she parroted in an exaggerated imitation of his voice.

Xander chuckled. "I don't sound anything like that. You doing the most."

She started saying something, but he raised his hands with his palm facing out and said, "Aye, porcupine. Chill."

He was so stupid calling her a porcupine, but the imagery made Navaya's cheek twitch. She hated that he could amuse her even when she didn't want to be. He poked her gently where her cheek was twitching. "Just go 'head and smile before you trip your circuit."

She chuckled. When she spoke again her voice was serious. "You hurt my feelings, though."

"Why?"

"Is this where I repeat that you called me unattractive."

"Stop that shit," he said. "You know you're hot as hell. I have to listen to Quinn and Jay go on about how much they love you. My girlfriends break up with me because they can't handle it. And I have two eyes in my head. It's got nothing to do with how attractive you are. I've just never thought of you... *like that*. Well, other than that one time in Aruba and lemme tell you... I've watched some fucked up porn that left me feeling less disgusted with myself than I did that time."

"Wait, what?"

He looked at her sheepishly. "You really want to get into *that* right now?"

"I'm not letting *that* slide so there's no time like the present," she said shrugging her shoulders slightly.

She could almost see Xander trying to think of a way to change the line of conversation but he gave up eventually. Navaya wasn't surprised. Xander knew her well enough to know she would badger the hell out of him until he satisfied her curiosity.

"Fine," he said. "But I'm gonna need some rum."

CHAPTER SIX

She was laughing again. Xander didn't mind too much that it was at his expense. He was just happy they were no longer having *that* conversation. He hated to see the embarrassment in Navaya's eyes. They didn't do awkwardness. They didn't do embarrassment. They were always transparent with each other, even if they didn't see eye to eye. Xander never once thought Navaya wouldn't have taken his comment the way he meant it. He'd underestimated just how much her ex fucked with her self-esteem. Unattractive? It annoyed him she would even think that. Navaya was bad as hell. If Xander got a dollar every time someone asked him how he managed to be best friends with a woman who looked like *that* without trying to shoot his shot, he'd be able to quit teaching and pursue the music career he wanted. But to Xander, her attractiveness was just an objective fact about her. Like the way she always smelled like warm vanilla, the way she was a hardened fries thief and the way she sometimes snorted while she laughed. He wasn't lying when he told her he didn't think about her sexually. Well, except that one time. He'd kept it a secret for eighteen years only to now be sitting on Navaya's couch, glass of rum in hand, listening to her snort for how hard she was laughing about it.

"That's wild," she said. She tried to sit up straight as she wiped the tears streaming down her cheek. "I remember that bathing suit too. It wasn't even revealing."

"I'd just turned thirteen, just started noticing breasts and you'd brushed all the way up on me while you were trying to get the beach ball. Man, I was just skinniness and hormones. I didn't know what to do with myself."

"So you told your mom you had diarrhea and ran back to the hotel room to jack off?" She took a deep breath before the laughter started again.

"Look," he said, trying to fight the smile tugging at his lips. "I was a kid. I just remember feeling guilty as fuck afterwards and I've never thought about you like that again. You been thinking about fucking me?"

The question knocked the laughter right out of Navaya. Her eyes went wide. "What the fuck? *No.*"

"You should see the horror on your face," he said. "Why did you think asking me for *mentordick* was a good idea considering you can't even stomach the abstract thought of me fucking you?"

"I thought it would be different once we got started," she admitted. "Sometimes attraction ignites like the strike of a match. Sometimes it's like rubbing sticks together until something sparks. They both burn just as hot."

Navaya shifted on the couch. "Look... I've already put it out there. Maybe we can just test it out?"

She tried to keep her voice casual, but Xander could tell there was nothing casual about her request. He was confident enough in his friendship with Navaya to know nothing could truly break their bond, but he still hesitated. When Navaya pulled her bottom lip through her teeth as she waited for his response, something different flared in Xander—curiosity. How would his body react if she'd been pulling her teeth through his lips instead? Maybe, like he suspected, it wouldn't, and he'd feel like he had after he came in that hotel room in Aruba. Or maybe, just maybe, they'd both explode.

"Tell me more about this test," he said eventually.

"Kiss me," Navaya said. A mischievous smile spread across her face. "I won't grade you *too* hard."

Xander shifted on the couch so they were close enough for their thighs to touch. "Is that a challenge?"

Navaya shrugged. "Do you accept?"

He brought his hand to her cheek, lightly brushing his thumb across her lips. He wanted to ask if she could remember a time when he turned down a challenge but he didn't. She'd probably dig up some obscure memory from when they were ten and then they'd get caught up with throwing teasing jabs back and forth until they lost whatever this moment was. Challenge or not, Xander wanted to see this shit through. He brought his forehead to hers, stalling for a few seconds. His thoughts were racing. Xander almost chuckled at how crazy that was. Why the fuck was he tripping over a kiss? Navaya's breathing was quick and shallow. The observation made him feel a bit better. At least he wasn't the only nervous one.

"Here goes nothing," he murmured, tipping her chin upward with his thumb and capturing her mouth with his. There were no sparks when he started kissing Navaya's soft, pliant lips. His heart didn't speed up. His dick didn't twitch. Everything was wrong. Their lips and teeth clashed, and every time one of them tried to adjust, somehow things got worse. He felt Navaya's laughter vibrating in her chest before it spilled from her mouth as she pulled away from him. Xander gave her a sheepish grin.

"Well..." he said.

"That was *not* it!" Her laughter was louder and more

raucous than before. Xander felt a type of way. He wasn't sure what he'd expected, but he hadn't been prepared for their attempt to fail so spectacularly. At least Navaya was finding the whole damn thing funny. Her shoulders heaved as she continued laughing. She reached down to the coffee table to grab her glass of wine when her cleavage almost spilled over the top of her tank top. Xander allowed his gaze to linger there for a few moments. He'd never done anything like that before and as he watched the perfect brown crescents of her breasts, Xander wondered why the fuck not. He tried to imagine what her breasts would look like if he reached forward and lifted the tank top. He was so caught up in his thoughts that he didn't notice Navaya's laughter had come to a spluttering halt. He tugged his gaze away and caught her eyes. "Two out of three?"

She gave him a small nod and Xander brought his hands to her breasts, caressing the globes that didn't quite fit in his palms before he gently pinched her nipples through the cotton fabric of the tank top. They hardened instantly. He pinched a bit harder and barely hid his smile at Navaya's sharp intake of air. He kept his gaze on her, watching her eyes widen and her lips part.

I want to know what faces she makes when she comes.

His fingers momentarily stalled as he recognized the absolute truth in the thought. Xander leaned forward and kissed her lips lightly before dragging his mouth across her cheek, jaw and down to her neck. He kissed her neck and then pulled her soft flesh between his teeth. It was her startled, husky cry that settled things in his mind. Xander Spencer was going to fuck his best friend.

CHAPTER SEVEN

Navaya's mind raced. Xander's warm hands slid up and down her back as he continued kissing her neck. She hated that it was so easy, but her pussy was already throbbing. She gasped when those warm hands covered her breasts and kneaded them with just enough pressure to have her leaning forward into his touch.

When Xander's lips found hers again, it was nothing like the first time. And Jesus Christ, she hadn't been ready. There was nothing awkward about how his lips moved roughly over hers as he coaxed her mouth open with his tongue. He continued tugging at her nipples as his tongue caressed hers. Her moans only seemed to spur him on more. His hands moved to her waist and suddenly he was tugging her on to his lap where his hardness pressed against her center. She gasped. Her university roommate hadn't just doing the most while Xander fucked her after all. He grabbed the back of her neck as he deepened the kiss and she instinctively rocked against his hardened dick. Her pussy purred with satisfaction. She continued grinding against him until she could feel her stomach tightening. When his hands went back to her waist, Navaya thought he was going to help speed up the orgasm building inside her. Xander didn't. He eased her off of his lap and lay her down on the couch. She bit her lip in anticipation. She was perfectly content with coming while grinding against the bulge in his sweatpants like it owed her something, but she was sure she would appreciate whatever he was about to do even more. He kissed her, biting into her lips before he pulled away and said, "Are you still interested in activating my *mentordick* program?"

Her pussy clenched as she arched towards him. "Yes, please."

Xander smirked. "We'll pick this up later."

He was standing before Navaya could process that her so-called best friend intended to leave her sprawled out on her couch with her nipples rock hard, pussy wet and pleading, on the verge of the orgasm she desperately needed.

"What the fuck, Xander?" she asked, pushing herself into an upright position. "Where are you going?"

He leaned down and dropped a kiss on her forehead. "To plan out my syllabus, Navi-Nav."

He winked at her and started adjusting his dick in his sweats. She growled his name when he actually started making his way to the door.

"I know you know how to take care of yourself," he shot over his shoulder as he continued down the hall. "I'll hit you up tomorrow."

Navaya was about to follow him to the door but stopped herself. She wasn't sure she could write a bestseller from jail. And, as much as her pussy protested playtime being cut short, Navaya had a feeling sex with Xander would be worth the wait.

CHAPTER EIGHT

Xander had noble intentions when he left Navaya lying on her couch nearly an hour before. She'd only asked him to have sex with her because she wanted inspiration for her writing. He planned to take his role as *Giver of Inspiring Dick* very seriously. So, although he knew he could have brought her to multiple orgasms with his fingers, tongue and dick, he wanted to leave her with the anticipation. Fuck noble intentions. His dick was swollen, throbbing and wanted to be buried deep in Navaya's wet sex. He squeezed his eyes shut at the thought of Navaya's body, slick with sweat, pressed up against him as her pussy clenched him tight. He tried again to distract his body with watching a rerun of the previous night's basketball game and finally felt himself regaining control. He was engrossed in the game when his cell phone chimed.

Navaya: We good, right? I don't want things to be weird.

Xander: We'll always be good.

He sent the message and his fingers hovered over the keyboard for a while. Eventually, he decided to be blunt and sent a follow-up message.

Xander: Tonight was… fun.

Navaya: Fun? You dipped just as I was about to get off. I'm mad as hell at you.

Xander: Leaving wasn't exactly easy for me, but it was necessary. All in good time, Navi-Nav.

Navaya: Whatever, Xan. I already took care of it myself.

Xander's dick twitched at the thought of Navaya making herself come. His phone chimed again but this time it was a video. His breath caught in his throat when he let it play. Navaya had positioned the camera to give a full view of her pussy. And what a pretty pussy it was.

"Jesus Christ," he murmured as he watched her flick her index finger over her swollen clit a few times before she dragged it down her slit and pushed it inside. She made a soft noise in her throat and Xander's dick stopped twitching. It went rock hard. Her hand disappeared out of the view of the camera and returned with a lime green vibrator. He watched the pink of her pussy stretch to accommodate it. Xander licked his lips. He couldn't wait to get his mouth on her. It was going to be a fucking feast. She withdrew the vibrator slowly, revealing just how much she'd coated it with her juices. Xander felt like a fucking fool. He'd been two minutes away from drowning in her wetness. His ass should've stayed. He sighed as she started pumping the vibrator in and out of her pussy, arching her back when she hit a spot she liked. She was moaning hard now, and Xander wished he could see her face. He figured he needed to take a page out of Navaya's book and *take care of it* himself since her pussy wasn't an option. He reached into his sweatpants and fisted the head of his dick, not at all surprised to find it already moist with pre-cum. He eased his sweatpants down and his dick sprung free. Xander's eyes were fixed on his phone's screen as he spat in his hand and wrapped it around the length of his dick. He tried to imagine being buried in Navaya as he stroked himself—lightly and then harder still, picking up speed as Navaya did on the screen. Her moans had become jagged screams as she moved the vibrator as fast as her hand would allow while the video started shaking. Xander smiled, imagining her hands shaking as she lost control. He tightened his fist and stroked as his balls tightened. Navaya thrust her hips upwards as her screams intensified. This time she dropped the phone altogether. Xander's head fell back and he closed his eyes while he continued his stroking. His eyes shot open when Navaya stopped screaming, "*oh my God*" and "*oh shit*" and screamed something he was intimately familiar with.

"Xander," she moaned. She called his name a few more times in that breathy, shaky voice before her moans became guttural again. Xander was barely holding it together, but hearing his name on her lips sent him straight over the edge. He was still struggling to catch his breath while he used his shirt to clean up the mess he'd made on his stomach. It took another few seconds before he could send a text.

Xander: **You wicked as shit for that.**

She sent back a smiley face and he found himself pulling up the video again. Xander sure as hell wasn't thirteen anymore. He thought he would die of shame the last time he masturbated to thoughts of Navaya. Thirty-one-year-old Xander felt no such thing. His dick began hardening again as he re-watched Navaya slide her finger into her pussy. All he felt now was anticipation and lust.

CHAPTER NINE

"You sent Xander *what?*" Tasha exclaimed loudly, clapping her hand over her mouth as she laughed. A few of the patrons in the Starbucks they popped into after their morning workout glanced in their direction.

"I sent him a three-minute video of me fucking myself with a lime green vibrator," Navaya said. She made a face. She wasn't mad about sending the video. He'd deserved it after the stunt he pulled. Navaya watched it over after she sent it and thought it was damn hot... until she caught the part that made her burn with embarrassment. She'd been so caught up in fantasizing about him that she'd screamed his name when she came. *Several times.* Tasha's giggle pulled her from her embarrassed thoughts. Navaya took a sip of her green tea.

"So y'all all in!" Tasha observed. "I didn't expect you to jump in with both feet like that. But then again, you never back down once you decide to go for something and Xander has always been chaotic. Y'all spoke today?"

Navaya waited a full ten seconds before she responded. "He sent me a dick pic and captioned it *your fave vibrator could never.*"

Navaya's pussy throbbed as she called to memory his dick. She sighed. It was dark enough that her mouth watered, wondering if it tasted like the chocolate it resembled. Thick and long enough that she knew he would hit all the right spots without trying. She smiled. If Xander's stroke game was on point, she'd be gone for.

"Eeey," Tasha yelled. A few more people glanced in their direction. "Xander is applying the pressure."

She lowered her voice and eased closer to Navaya. "Let sis see that dick."

Navaya almost spat out the tea she'd just taken a sip of. "Tash! I'm not sneaking you a look. Imagine him showing Cole that video I sent him."

Tasha's eyes sparkled the way they usually did whenever Cole came up in conversation. She smirked. "I wouldn't mind Cole getting a glimpse of my goodies."

"You're married!"

Tasha made a face. "I doubt for much longer."

Navaya asked Tasha what was going on, but she wasn't having any of it. She continued talking about Xander as if Navaya hadn't said anything at all.

"I love how you can talk about Xander showing Cole the video with a hundred percent confidence he would never do it. That kind of trust is dope."

Navaya chuckled. "I trust Xander with my life."

He was one of only a few people she trusted and depended on without reservation.

Tasha's smirk widened. "That's why he was the perfect choice to turn that pussy out. You're about to get your mojo back."

"It'd be crazy if this actually works."

"Trust me, it will," Tasha said. "The question is where you

gonna go from here if he really gives you the best fuck of your life."

"What do you mean?"

"How would you go back to keeping your hands... and *other places* to yourself?"

Navaya paused. She'd done a list of pros and cons but never thought to consider what would happen if they actually liked this. She massaged her temple. Was this a bad idea? Were they making a mistake?

"Dead that right now."

Tasha's soft voice pulled her from her spiraling thoughts. "Huh?"

"I should've kept my mouth shut. Don't go panicking yourself out of a good time. I mean... you *have* been hella uptight for a while. I'm just sorry it took a hit to your career for you to pay attention."

"Why didn't you tell me?"

Tasha sucked her teeth. "Bitch, what do you think all those blind dates were about? I was trying to get your uptight ass some but you kept sending the niggas back unfucked."

Navaya laughed loudly. "Girl, please go before I get kicked out of this establishment without getting any work done."

She and Tasha spoke for a few more minutes before her friend grabbed her handbag and left after making Navaya promise to give her the dirty details later.

Navaya returned to her work in progress and spent some time rereading her scenes before she realized the current novel was going the way of the last. She fiddled for a few hours before she accepted the inevitable. Her stomach tightened into knots as she dragged the document to her computer's trashcan and cleared it before she lost her nerve. *Gone.* Nearly forty thousand words. She inhaled deeply and tried to focus on her breathing to fight away the panic that was making her head light. She needed to trust the process. She was halfway through a breath when her phone vibrated. Xander's name flashed across the screen.

"Hey," she said, closing her laptop and starting to shove it into her bag.

"Why do you sound like you're about to have a panic attack?" Xander asked. His voice was warm and laced with concern.

"I just deleted the novel I'm working on. Not some paragraphs. Not a chapter or two. The entire thing."

"Why would you do that?"

She sighed. "It was just as bland and boring as the last."

She knew she needed a clean slate, but Navaya was already regretting her impulsive decision.

"Stop overthinking it," Xander suggested. "You made the right decision. I'm going to swing by your apartment at six. I'm taking you out for something to eat."

Navaya wanted to ask Xander when exactly their *mentordick* arrangement would start but she stopped herself. *Go with the flow.*

"What should I wear?" she asked instead.

She could hear the laughter in his voice when he finally answered.

"Something that will hide wetness well."

CHAPTER TEN

Xander glanced at his watch as he shoved his feet into his Jordans and picked up the box on his bed. Navaya was punctual as hell and he needed to get to her before she started getting dressed. He grinned when he thought of the surprise he had for her. He was about twenty minutes away from seeing just how down Navaya was with this little project of theirs. Xander liked to think he knew Navaya better than he knew himself, but he couldn't decide which way he thought she'd lean. Would she go along with it or would she throw the box right back in his face? They were in for an interesting night. Navaya was sitting in her living room flipping through channels on the TV when he let himself into her apartment. She'd pulled her box braids into a bun but she was still wearing her bathrobe.

"Why are you so early?" she asked. Her forehead crinkled as she turned to look at him properly.

"I needed to catch you before you got dressed." He stepped forward and handed her the box. "I've got something for you to wear."

Her frown deepened. She took the box from him and inspected it as if the unmarked black box could give her any clues. She turned it over in her hands and shook it lightly before she asked, "What's this?"

"A vibrator."

"A vibrator?"

He nodded. "A vibrator."

"You brought me a vibrator... to wear?"

"All the instructions are inside." He checked his watch. "We got to get going soon if we're going to beat traffic."

She hesitated for just a second too long and Xander thought she would refuse. But she didn't.

"A vibrator to wear?" she whispered to herself as she got up from the couch. She gave him another puzzled look before she made her way down the hall. Xander felt himself harden as he watched her go. He wondered which one of them would crack before the end of the night.

A VIBRATOR.

Xander bringing a vibrator for her to wear should have set off warning bells in Navaya's mind. It didn't. It intrigued her. And turned her on a little bit too. She pulled the vibrator from the box. *Lovense Lush.* She turned the pink, bulbous part of the vibrator between her fingers before she decided it was time to get down to business. Xander had placed a small bottle of lube in the box with a note that read '*in case this makes it easier*' but she didn't need it. Her pussy, already slick with her wetness, accepted the vibrator easily. She took a few minutes to steady herself before she pulled on the black jeans and slouchy yellow sweater she'd chosen.

Xander was leaned up against the wall when she got back to the living room. She pulled her lips between her teeth as she took in how the white, Oxford shirt stretched across his chest and his muscular biceps. His sessions with Cole were definitely paying off. He gave her a once over and then asked, "You wearing it?"

She started to answer but before she could, Xander swiped his phone screen and Navaya's legs almost gave out. She tried to grab the wall as the sharp vibrations caused her pussy to clench the vibrator she'd pushed deep inside her. Xander bit the corner of his bottom lip and smirked widely. "Damn. That was better than I expected it to be."

Navaya tried to find words, but she couldn't. After a while, she managed to get out through clenched teeth. "Oh my God."

She squeezed her eyes shut as she clenched her thighs together, desperate to stop the overwhelming sensations flooding her body. She hadn't known what to expect, but it definitely wasn't *that*. Her pussy pulsed as pleasure pooled deep in her belly. It was too much... too soon, and if Navaya had been controlling the vibrator, she would've stopped it to give herself time to recover. As it was, the vibrating pattern began changing —hard and then whisper soft, deep pulses and then rapid flicks. She bit her lips and the moan she'd been trying to hold finally escaped. She tried to lean her body against the wall, but her knees kept buckling. Navaya couldn't pull enough air into her lungs to catch her breath. She brought her hand to the crotch of her jeans and pressed hard against her swollen clit, desperate to soothe the aching she felt there even as the vibrations inside her drove her closer to the edge. And then it stopped. Her pussy mourned the loss of vibrations almost immediately. Xander was grinning at her so widely that Navaya wanted to smack the smugness from his face. Her body slowly stopped shaking, and she could finally string together a few coherent thoughts. It hit her at once that Xander planned to take her out to eat with this *thing* inside her. Xander's grin widened when he noticed her realizing what he had planned for their evening out. Navaya shook her head and laughed. "No way. You're crazy if you think I'm going to agree to this."

Xander pushed himself off the wall and crossed the short distance to her. He wrapped a hand around her waist and pulled her into him. "Sometimes you gotta let go control for a while."

His breath was warm against her cheek and her damned pussy reacted instantly. She clenched around the vibrator, setting off another round of unexpected pleasure. She pressed herself into him, trying to keep herself upright.

"I'm not trying to embarrass myself in public."

His hand moved lower and cupped her ass as his mouth sought hers. There was no hesitation this time around. He explored her mouth with the same urgency she felt. She pushed her body even closer to him as her hands found the back of his head and pulled him into her. He squeezed her ass and pulled her against the bulge in his pants. She moaned. There was no way they were doing whatever the hell Xander thought they had planned. She needed Xander deep inside her. And she needed it now.

Navaya pulled away from the kiss. "We're not going anywhere, Xan. I need you to fuck me. Now."

CHAPTER ELEVEN

He was out of his damn mind. There was nothing else that could explain how Xander was able to look at Navaya staring up at him with lust blazing in her eyes as she demanded he fuck her and say no. As horny as he was and as hard as he was, Xander was surprised he found the self-control. Xander adjusted himself in his jeans while a scowling Navaya retreated to her bedroom for her shoes. He was playing the long game. But would he survive it? He wondered if she truly realized that this would be harder for him than it would be for her. Literally. Xander pulled out his phone and opened the app linked to the vibrator. He ran his finger across the screen in up and down motions and chuckled under his breath when he heard a sharp yelp coming from the direction of Navaya's bedroom. She glowered at him when she returned.

"Promise me you won't overdo it, Xander," she said. She came to stand in front of him and placed one hand on her hip. Damn, she was cute when she was irritated.

"Trust me a little, Nav," he said. "The whole point of this is for you to let go control."

"You calling me wound up?"

Xander smiled but didn't respond. He wasn't going to allow her to draw him into that argument even though that was exactly what he was saying. Navaya was the most in control person he'd ever met in his life. It wouldn't surprise him if she'd done a pros and cons list, a flowchart and a venn diagram before she decided to throw out the *mentordick* idea. Navaya planned her life in five-year increments from the time they were thirteen years old and almost everything went just the way she planned it. Well, except Callahan. Callahan definitely didn't go the way Navaya planned. Nor was stalling at this point in her career. They'd settled into his car as he began the drive to Falls Church. He figured taking her to one of their favorite restaurants would make up for the way he planned to tease her all night. He glanced over at his usually assured best friend sitting stiffly with her hands clasped on her lap. Xander reached over and squeezed her thigh—something he'd probably done a thousand times before. This time electricity surged through him. She looked up at him with wide eyes and flicked her tongue across her lip. He took a breath. He wanted to reach over and pull her lips into his mouth as his hands slid under her sweater to touch her warm skin. He shifted in his seat, hoping to take the edge off the discomfort. *The long game, Xander*, he tried to remind himself. Except, his body wasn't paying attention at all.

She ached. Navaya squeezed her thighs together as she tried to concentrate on the scenery whizzing by as they made their way out of Maryland towards Virginia. She needed to focus on something, *anything*, other than Xander sitting next to her. He was *too* close. She was noticing Xander in ways she hadn't over the course of more than three decades. How was that even possible? She watched his big hands gripping the steering wheel and imagined those hands cupping her ass, squeezing her breasts, grabbing her throat and yanking her hair. She clenched her thighs together again, harder this time. Her pussy clenched around the bulbous head of the vibrator still inside her. Navaya bit her lip, hard, to prevent ragged moans from escaping her mouth. She saw Xander smirk out of the corner of her eye.

"This funny to you?" she asked. There was attitude in her voice, but she didn't care. She was... frustrated. Navaya couldn't remember the last time every single cell in her body craved someone's lips... fingertips... dick. She couldn't remember ever being so riled up with sexual frustration that she wanted to scream... or cry. She'd never had to wait for sex. Foreplay with Callahan was him doing *just enough*. *Just enough* to get her turned on *just enough* for her to be *just wet enough* for his dick to slide in easily. She tried to think of a scene where any character in her books were about to come out of their skin with need. And even if they had... how effectively could she write about someone losing sexual control when she never experienced it before. Definitely not like this. Not in a way that had her wondering how well Xander could drive with her lips wrapped around his dick. Xander didn't answer her question right away. He reached for her hand and guided it to his crotch where his erection strained against his jeans.

"As I've said before, this ain't easy for me either."

He glanced off the road and looked at her for a few seconds before he added. "At least you'll get to release some tension before we're done with dinner."

He smiled. "Several times."

CHAPTER TWELVE

Xander loved Hot and Juicy Crawfish. It was the one place he and Navaya never argued about eating at. That alone was worth the fifty minute drive out to Virginia. The amazing crab legs and mussels Navaya couldn't get enough of was an added bonus. The server guided them to a booth near the back of the restaurant. Xander chose Hot and Juicy Crawfish for more than just the food. The restaurant had booths available and was bathed in muted lights which gave an added air of privacy even though they would be in plain view. The servers were attentive but not in the pop up every three minutes kind of way. He was going to need that. He slid into the same side of the booth as Navaya instead of sitting opposite her like he usually did. He met her questioning gaze with a smile. "I'm just using my body to block yours. This isn't about embarrassing you. It's all about your pleasure." Her mouth parted. Xander leaned forward and kissed her even though he knew touching her would make things even harder for him. Her lips, soft and plump, moved over his as she ran her tongue lightly across his teeth. His hand found the back of her neck and he pressed his lips harder against hers. He sucked her bottom lip into his mouth before biting it gently. He

felt Navaya shift in the booth, angling her body towards him
and he knew he had to end things before neither of them could
stop. It was hard, though. She felt so good in his arms that
Xander wanted to help her along on to his lap. A timid *"Are you
ready to order?"* had them pulling away from each other like
they'd been burned. Navaya was looking everywhere except at
the young, skinny black guy who didn't look a day over eighteen.
Xander couldn't decide if he was happy for the interruption or
annoyed by it. He glanced at the young man's name-tag. Sean
needed to learn to read the fucking room. Xander unclenched
his jaw and thanked Sean for the menus.

"Kinda sucks when you're forced to stop just as you're
getting into it, doesn't it?" Navaya said with a chuckle as she
accepted the menu he handed to her.   Xander laughed.
"Touché."

They placed orders for mussels, lobster, snow crab legs and
fries before they moved on to drinks as if they didn't order the
same thing every time. He had his usual craft beer and Navaya
ordered the margarita flight. Xander tried to diffuse the sexual
tension between them by telling Navaya about three girls in his
class he was trying to raise money to send to a programming
camp for the summer.

"They're so bright," he said, taking a sip of his beer. "And
you know that little black girls are often left out when it comes
to STEM."

"Have you spoken to the school?"

He fixed her with a look that made her chuckle. Of course
he had, but the administration had a problem with him singling
out the girls. If he wanted the school's budget to be used to send
students to camp, then the process needed to be 'fair'. He
related the conversation he'd had with the principal—a thin,
balding white man who often used air quotes when he spoke
about affirmative action.

"I just shut it down," he said. "Fuck that shit. I'll get it done on my own."

Navaya nodded as she reached into the sauce-drenched bag they served the mussels in to pull out another mussel.

"Count me in," she said as she popped one in her mouth. "I'll give a couple hundred and force Tasha to join me."

Xander grinned. He expected nothing less from Navaya. She always supported everything important to him. It was as simple as showing up to every single gig he had even though she must have heard each variation of the band's set a hundred times. She was always down for an adventure. She was his therapist, relationship expert and a swift kick up his ass whenever he needed one. She was central to every important aspect of his life. He jokingly referred to her as his soul mate but without the messy addition of sexual attraction. He had meant it too. Well, sexual attraction had just joined the chat and its intensity surprised the hell out of Xander. Had the switch just been waiting to be flipped all this time? Xander was too busy trying to deal with his new physical reactions to consider the insane scenarios running through his mind as he glanced over at Navaya. He didn't like the direction of his thoughts, so he reached for his phone and opened the Lovense remote. He felt Navaya stiffen beside him. She gasped when he made a wavy pattern with his index finger on the screen. He traced the pattern again and smiled when she began squirming. He did it again. And again. And again. Navaya bit into her bottom lip and her eyes started fluttering shut. He shifted in the booth. This damn torture went both ways.

"You're doing great," he soothed, squeezing her thigh. He resisted the urge to reach between her legs and cup her sex. Barely. It was a good thing too, because Sean showed up, perky as hell, wanting to know if they needed a refill on their drinks a few seconds later.

"Damn it, Sean," he muttered under his breath before he turned to the young man and asked for another round just to send him on his way.

"You should probably stop until he brings the drinks back," Navaya panted.

"You're right," he said. "It's kind of obvious I'm up to something, isn't it?"

She nodded so vigorously her box braids shook and Xander smiled. She was so fucking beautiful. Relief flooded her face when he placed his phone face down on the table but it quickly faded with a sharp gasp. Xander smiled.

"It comes with pre-programming," he whispered. "I've set it to *earthquake*."

If looks could kill. Navaya moaned quietly, reaching out to grip the table. Xander felt like a voyeur as he watched her react to the sensations the vibrator produced. She closed her eyes as her breaths became unsteady. He didn't miss the tiny roll of her hips and arch in her lower back as she ground against the seating. She clasped her hands and squeezed them together as she looked up at him with wide, pleading eyes. He brought his hand to her lower back and massaged her gently. Xander leaned into her and whispered. "Just let go."

His dick throbbed just thinking about finally seeing what Navaya would look like as she came. She shook her head. "No. I can't. Not here..."

"Yes you can," he said, continuing to rub her back. Her eyes started watering as she shook her head again just as Sean returned with the drinks.

He placed them awkwardly on the table as Navaya gasped and squeezed her eyes shut. The young man started to ask if everything was okay but one look from Xander sent him scurrying away. He'd spent a lot of time thinking about how Navaya would *look* as she came. Would she keep her eyes open or would she squeeze them shut? Would her lips part or would she bite them? Would her nostrils flare? He realized now he didn't give any consideration to whether she'd be quiet or loud. As he watched her lips fall open and her body shake, Xander knew she'd be loud as fuck.

"Hey," he whispered, reaching out for her. "I got you. Just let go."

He kissed her hard, swallowing her mewling cries as her body succumbed to the orgasm. Xander kept his lips pressed to hers in an open-mouthed kiss until her body finally stopped shaking. Her eyes were moist and her skin dewy. Xander's breath caught in his throat. He'd planned to take her home and kiss her goodnight, but he knew he didn't have it in him anymore. Fuck the long game.

CHAPTER THIRTEEN

Navaya glanced around the restaurant as her cheeks flamed with embarrassment. She was so sure all the other patrons and staff would be staring at them but was surprised to find everybody minding their own business. She was shook. There was no way in hell nobody noticed that she was over there having the most intense orgasm she'd had in a long ass time.

"You good?"

Xander searched her face as if he was expecting her to flip out on him. She nodded. Good? She was amazing. Her limbs were warm and loose, and she felt the kind of lightheaded endorphin rush that usually required an hour of cardio at the gym.

"Let's get out of here?" She tried to keep her voice casual, but she knew she might actually flip out on him if he resisted. Her orgasm had been explosive but she still ached to have him buried to the hilt inside her. She felt wild with desperation. He surprised her by reaching for his wallet and signaling to Sean that he was ready for the bill. Navaya took the time to head to the restroom on slightly unsteady feet. She thought of emptying her bladder but had no clue how she would navigate the vibrator situation, so she just splashed some water over her face and took a good look at herself in the bathroom mirror. Damn. She looked as desperate as she felt. Xander was signing his credit card slip when she returned to the table. He looked up, caught her eyes and smiled at her. Her stomach somersaulted a little as she imagined how those lips would feel on her body… how those teeth would feel grazing her nipples. She took a deep breath and tried to center herself. It didn't do a lot of good. The last time Navaya remembered feeling so out of control was when she and Xander ate twice the recommended amount of edibles because they weren't feeling the effects as quickly as they wanted. Xander reached for her hand when she was close enough as he rose from where he sat. His warm palm against hers sent shock waves down her spine. She giggled. This was ridiculous.

"What's so funny?"

Xander traced circles on the inside of her wrist with his thumb as they approached the parking lot.

"I feel like I'm in some edible induced dream. Or I've woken up in some alternate universe where you're a tree I'm getting ready to climb."

She blushed when Xander licked his lips and chuckled. "What kinda tree you thinking about? A shrub or a coconut tree? Just wanna know if I need to be offended."

Laughter spilled from Navaya's lips. "When will you learn to behave?"

He caught her waist and pulled her close. "Definitely not tonight."

Xander grasped her cheek and pulled her into him, capturing her lips in his as she sighed. Her hands grabbed the back of his head and pulled him closer. She'd known this man for over thirty years and she never imagined that his lips would move so perfectly against hers. Or that it'd feel so damn good being pressed against his body. Her eyes fluttered closed as he palmed her ass with both hands and jerked her against his hard on. They were leaned up against his car and Navaya didn't care that people might wander out into the parking lot and see them going at it. She grabbed one of his hands from its position on her ass and pushed it under her sweater. She moaned and ground herself against him when he squeezed her breast before slipping two fingers into the top of her bra to pinch her nipple. Navaya wasn't sure how long they stayed there, pressed up against the car in a haze of lust until loud wolf whistles pulled them apart.

"Get it, get it," a burly brother with locs yelled as he and his girl walked past the car hand in hand. Navaya caught Xander's eyes and they burst out laughing. Everything was so damned easy and comfortable with him. A jolt of panic shot through her when she remembered what Tasha had to say about this possibly changing the dynamics of their relationship. She rested a hand against the hard planes of Xander's chest, wishing she could just take in how fast his heart was beating because he craved her. As it stood, Navaya had a question she needed answered.

"Promise me we'll be good after all of this," she whispered.

"Hey," he said. "We'll always be good. You ain't ever getting rid of me."

She grinned at him. "I can't even tell if that's a good thing."

Xander leaned forward and brushed his lips lightly against hers. "Let's get out of here, huh? I heard I've got a tree you're desperate to climb."

CHAPTER FOURTEEN

Xander didn't know how he made it back to Maryland with his sanity intact. Navaya kept her hand on his thigh during the entire drive and the scent of her sex filled the car's confined space. Every breath he took made his dick harder, yet he couldn't get enough of her. Tonight had been all about getting Navaya to lose control, but he ended up being the one on the verge of losing his mind. The brief walk from where he parked his car to Navaya's building could have lasted an hour for how impatient he was. Xander was tempted to lean into her and slide his hand under her sweater so he could feel the smooth expanse of her skin once they got into the elevator, but he restrained himself. There would be no stopping him once he finally got his hands on her. Navaya barely turned the lock on her apartment's door before he was on her. He held the back of her neck and thrust his tongue into her mouth, running it across the inside of her lips as she wrapped a leg around his waist. He pivoted on one foot so he could press her against the same door she'd just closed. Kissing Navaya was indescribable. He chuckled against her lips when he remembered how bad their first kiss had been. He was happy they gave it another go because he would have never known the absolute pleasure it was to devour Navaya's mouth. She pushed herself hard against him, straining to get even closer as he sucked her top lip into his mouth while his hand went for the zipper on her jeans. He couldn't wait. He needed to know if her pretty pussy tasted just as sweet. Xander kneeled in front of her, helping her take off the ankle boots she wore before helping her wriggle out of her jeans. He spread her legs just about shoulder width before he buried his face between her thighs. Her intoxicating scent hit him in heady waves and Xander stayed motionless for a few seconds just inhaling her. He pinched the end of the vibrator and gently let it slide out of Navaya. It glistened with her wetness. Xander let it fall to the floor before turning his attention back to the beauty in front of him. He swiped his tongue slowly up her slit. Navaya shivered. Xander held on to her thighs to steady her as he plunged his tongue into her pussy. He tensed his tongue and flicked it against her clit a few times, enjoying the way she moaned and tried to squirm away from him. He savored Navaya's juices on his tongue. They could let him loose in a candy store for a decade and Xander was sure he wouldn't find candy that tasted as sweet as her pussy. He strummed her clit with his tongue as she arched her back, pushing his face deeper into her sex. He groaned into her warmth. Her breath caught in her throat as Xander went to work on her in earnest. He licked, nibbled, slurped and lavished attention on Navaya's sex until her body shook uncontrollably and her screams increased in fervor and pitch. She held on to the back of his head and alternated between pulling him closer and pushing him away. His dick pressed uncomfortably against his jeans but Xander didn't care. He could lose himself in Navaya's soft, sweetness forever. He settled into a rhythm that drew frantic cries from Navaya's throat. Her body tightened as Xander drew her clit into his mouth and sucked it.

Then, she fell apart. He didn't let up even as she gushed on his tongue.

"Please," she whined. "I can't. No more."

Xander brushed his lips against her throbbing pussy as he reluctantly stopped devouring her. He pulled himself into a standing position, wrapping his hand around her waist and drawing her still shaking body into his embrace. Her eyes were wild with lust when she finally pulled away. She tiptoed, locked her hands behind his neck and yanked his lips to hers. The kiss was filled with all the franticness he felt. Xander needed to get Navaya to a surface, *any surface*, so he could sink into her. She stepped back and stared up at him as she pulled her sweater over her head and deftly unhooked her bra. His gaze lingered on her smooth brown breasts with their upturned nipples as her chest heaved while she struggled to catch her breath. She reached for his jeans and started unbuckling his belt.

"Is this out of control enough for you?" she panted. She pushed her hand down his pants and began stroking him. Xander jerked against her touch, unprepared for just how good it felt to have her warm hands slowly pumping him. He drew her into another searing kiss. Xander rest his cheek against hers, struggling to keep his composure as her strokes got faster.

"Navi-Nav," he groaned. "I gotta be inside you."

"Finafuckingly," she whispered. She helped him get the rest of his clothes off. They fell into a heap on the floor beside her jeans, sweater, panties and bra. Xander began to suggest they moved things into the living room but barely got the words out of his mouth before Navaya reached for his dick again. She wrapped a leg around his waist as she guided him inside her hot, slick pussy. He thrust into her hard, pushing them back against the door. Navaya held on to his shoulder, drawing her nails down his back as he steadied one hand around her waist and the other against the door while he thrust into her over and over again. She felt good. So fucking good. Too fucking good. He slowed his movements when he felt the familiar tightening in his thighs and balls. Xander didn't care how hard he had to fight. He wasn't going to nut quickly. His lips roamed aggressively over hers as he picked back up his thrusting. Xander groaned into her neck, hands slipping from her waist to cup her ass. He'd started losing the fight when Navaya dug her nails so deeply into his shoulders that he winced in pain. Her eyes widened slightly before she squeezed them shut as her lips parted.

"Xander," she whispered throwing her head back as her body began shaking again and her pussy clenched him so tightly that he started feeling lightheaded. He followed close behind her with a curse on his lips, barely able to keep them upright as the orgasm ripped through his body. It seemed to go on forever but when he could finally produce a coherent thought Xander realized that things between them would never, *could never*, be the same.

CHAPTER FIFTEEN

Navaya would have collapsed right there on the floor if Xander wasn't holding her upright. Her orgasm came in waves and each time she thought she'd exhausted the pleasure that made her knees buckle, another wave crashed over her. Her sex throbbed hard as she finally disentangled herself from Xander's arms. She couldn't seem to catch her breath. Her legs still shook when she made her way into the kitchen and poured a glass of water. She swallowed it in one gulp before she smiled sheepishly at Xander, who'd followed behind her, and asked him if he needed a glass. He declined but pressed himself up behind her and placed a kiss at her nape. His dick was hard against her ass and made it very clear that he wanted to go another round. Her pussy throbbed on cue to remind her that she wanted that other round too. His lips moved from the base of her neck towards her shoulder, pulling her skin between his teeth. Navaya arched into him when those big hands ran up her thighs, over her stomach and grabbed her breasts. He kneaded them, grasping her hardened nipples between his index and middle fingers and rubbing them until she cried out. She spun around so she could face Xander. She'd expected the almost feral desire she felt to have lessened now that she'd had her release... multiple times. But somehow it still burned hot like lava. She crashed her mouth against his and lost herself in the feel of his lips moving hungrily against hers before she pulled back and smiled at him.

"Maybe we can make it to the bed this time?"

He chuckled and her stomach contracted at the sexy, husky sound. "Lead the way."

He smacked her ass as she turned toward her bedroom.

"Baby got back," he laughed and soon she was giggling with him. Xander could still make her giggle like a schoolgirl even though she felt like her entire body would combust with need. He sat back on the bed and pulled her into him.

"I promised to give you something to climb," he teased. She started laughing, but the laughter was replaced with a moan when he slid two fingers inside her. He pumped his fingers in and out of her sex as he massaged her clit with his thumb. Navaya's head fell forward as tiny, sharp jolts of pleasure passed through her body. She'd never felt anything like that before. It wasn't an orgasm even though it took her breath away. It was like her body was waiting... preparing... gearing up... for the most intense pleasure of her life. Navaya shivered just thinking about it. She straddled Xander, kneeling on either side of him on the bed as his dick pressed against the entrance of her pussy. She breathed in deeply as she sank down on him. Then, with her hands on his shoulders, she rode him. She let her head fall backwards as she determined to do exactly what Xander had asked her to do all night. She finally released the reins on control. She refused to feel self conscious about the bit of fat forming a small pouch on her lower belly, or the love handles that Xander seemed to enjoy grabbing on to. She cast aside any thoughts about whether the slow, lazy rhythm she'd settled into was doing it for Xander. It was doing it for her! In those moments all that mattered was the way his dick sliding in and out of her felt a little better every time she sank back down on him. The way his teeth grazed against her collarbone. The way the scents of their sweat, their sex and his spicy sandalwood cologne combined in a sensual symphony that left her head spinning and her body aching for more of him. Navaya sought Xander's mouth and moaned when her lips finally connected with his. She wanted to feel him everywhere. They were joined so closely she couldn't tell where he finished and she began, but that wasn't enough. Their skin, slick with sweat, slid against each causing beads of pleasure to erupt each time her hardened nipples glided against his chest, but that wasn't enough. His fingers alternated between digging into her ass and brushing down her spine, but that wasn't enough. When she buried her head into his neck as her body convulsed hard with the orgasm that seemed like it had been building forever, Navaya knew nothing *would* be enough. She grinned at him mischievously. She'd just have to settle for a few more rounds.

CHAPTER SIXTEEN

Depleted.

Xander thought he was made of the sturdy stuff. But he had never, *ever* had anyone push him to the brink like Navaya had. He'd given up on counting how many times they had sex somewhere between the third and fourth time she'd roused him from sleep with her lips around his dick. Things had been... explosive. Except, explosive seemed like too tame of a word to explain all that went down between him and Navaya. *Nuclear.* His lips curved into a smile as he called to mind some of the things they'd gotten up to. Yes. Nuclear was the perfect way to describe it. He was happy he'd scheduled their session for a Friday night. There was no way he'd have been any good to his students if he had to teach. Not with memories of Navaya's wet heat and soft lips playing in his head on repeat. Not when his dick was already hard as fuck even though he'd been buried deep in Navaya less than two hours before. He wasn't even sure when he'd fallen asleep, but he awoke to find Navaya's side of the bed empty. He interlocked his fingers and stretched his hands above his head, wincing at his soreness. Damn. He was getting old. He'd have to remember that. All night marathon sex sessions would not be as easy to recover from as when he was in his early twenties. Yet, he regretted nothing.

He found Navaya in her kitchen stirring something in a frying pan. She'd put on a silk teddy that rode up exposing a bit of her ass cheek when she turned to grab seasoning from the cupboard above the stove. His dick reacted violently as if he hadn't seen that bare ass in all its glory a few hours before.

"You gonna just stay there staring or say something?"

She turned from the stove and flashed him a big, bright smile that caused his heart to splutter in his chest. He paused for a few seconds. What the fuck was that?

"Lemme creep in peace," he said when his bearings returned. He crossed the space between them and pulled her against him before placing a small kiss on her neck. She melted into his embrace.

"Something smells great," he said. "Made enough for two?"

She rolled her eyes and went back to sautéing the cubed potatoes, diced sausages, onions and bell peppers. "I was planning on whipping up something for me, but I figured breakfast was the *least* I could do for you after your faithful service last night."

"I aim to please," he teased. "But you could have warned me you were insatiable."

Her laughter rang out like music, and Xander chuckled too.

"For real though, Navi-Nav. We were not ready."

He glanced down to his dick happily bobbing away, so she knew exactly what he was talking about.

"It's been a while," she said. "I guess I didn't realize how much I missed a good fuck until I had one."

He smirked. "A good fuck, huh?"

Navaya rolled her eyes and smacked him with the kitchen towel she'd been using to remove the frying pan from the stove. "Stop fishing for compliments with your conceited ass."

Things were normal as hell between them, even though he was buck ass naked, and Xander wasn't sure how he felt about that. He made them coffee as they chatted about their respective plans for the day. Although he wanted to head back to his apartment and crawl his depleted ass into bed, he had to meet up with Cole and the rest of the band to run through their set for their next gig the following month. It was the biggest venue they'd ever played in and Xander was eager to make sure they got everything just right. Navaya's Saturday plans were the same as always: yoga, reading, perhaps some writing before catching a matinee at the Imax in Silver Spring. Their easy conversation continued all the way through breakfast until Xander glanced at his watch and realized he really had to go if he didn't want to keep Cole waiting. Navaya cleaned up the table as he hunted for his clothes where they'd discarded them right in front of the front door the night before. She walked him to the door and Xander hesitated in the doorway for a few seconds, not quite sure about his next move. Navaya decided for him. She tiptoed and placed a kiss that should have been short and sweet against his lips, except he sank into her, teasing the seams of her lips with his tongue before deepening the kiss. She smiled when she finally pulled away languidly with lust in her eyes. She promised to text him later and hesitated just a few seconds before she shut the door. Xander leaned his back against the door and waited for his heart rate to return to normal. If this had been any other woman, he'd have walked away thinking this might be the start of something explosive. He couldn't remember the last time he'd ever connected with anyone sexually like that. He *had never* connected with anyone sexually like that. He rested his head against the closed door and shook his head. *What the fuck was going on?*

CHAPTER SEVENTEEN

Navaya leaned against the door she just closed and placed her hand to her chest. Her heart seemed to be trying to fight its way out of her body. What the *fuck* was going on? Good dick and several orgasms. Was that really all it took to turn her into a blubbering mess? A small smile crept across her face. *Good dick* was underselling Xander. Sex with Xander was ri*dick*ulously good. It hadn't been the sex or the orgasms or the *mentordick* agreement that stayed on her mind during breakfast that morning, though. She'd been thinking about just how damned cozy it all was. Navaya and Xander had shared breakfast more times than she could count. They'd shared beds often too. But they'd never had breakfast while they both still sizzled with the passion they'd tried, but failed, to work out the night before. She'd never watched Xander eat and feel herself get wet imagining those lips curved around her breasts... or clit... or pressed tenderly against her mouth. Navaya massaged her temples as if the action would get rid of the thoughts swirling around her head. She started to laugh after a few seconds. The next few weeks were going to be interesting as hell but that was what she got for opening Pandora's box.

NAVAYA WANTED to grab another cup of coffee and curl up on her couch so she could overthink every touch, every electrical current that shot through her body and the weird foreign flutters in her stomach whenever Xander crossed her mind. Crossed her mind. Ha! Xander *stayed* on her mind. She hadn't been able to sink into her couch because she was already almost late for her yoga class, but Xander remained heavy on her thoughts. She didn't miss the few quizzical looks Breanna shot her when she struggled to get into poses she usually repeated with ease. It didn't matter how many times she tried to focus. She couldn't. A small smile tugged at the corner of her mouth as she called to memory Xander covering her mouth with his as she screamed out her pleasure when her orgasm overtook her in their favorite booth at Hot and Juicy Crawfish. She stayed in *savasana* for a few more minutes than she usually did, allowing the small bits of inspiration that tugged at her mind from that memory to take firm roots. She couldn't remember the last time a scene popped into her mind, unbidden but so full of texture and life that she wanted to pull herself up into a sitting position and scribble it down right there on her yoga mat. As it was, Navaya rushed through showering and pulling back on comfy clothes. She quickly crossed the road to the Target and grabbed the first notebook she could find and a stack of pens. She was notorious for browsing for an ungodly amount of time before she decided on notebooks. So, that she grabbed the first thing her hands could reach said a lot for just how desperate she was to get her thoughts on paper. The desperation was very much like the desperation she'd felt the night before to have Xander all over and all up in her body, but it didn't burn quite the same. She made a quick detour to the Starbucks to grab a chai latte before she settled around a table in the courtyard. Navaya opened the book, popped in her headphones, put pen to paper and wrote.

"Ow."

Navaya clenched and unclenched her hand, hoping to soothe the cramping ache she felt. She reached for the latte and was shocked to find it had gone cold. How long had she been writing? She glanced at her watch and gasped. She'd be writing for over two-and-a-half hours. She started turning the pages backwards, flabbergasted at how much she wrote. Navaya chuckled. She hoped like hell the words that stared up at her from the pages in uneven, loopy scrawls made sense once she reread them. But she didn't want to do that just yet. She wanted to bask in the joy that unfurled in the pit of her stomach. It was the giddy excitement that she always felt when she'd broken a writing drought. Navaya took another sip of her now cold latte and tried to imagine Xander's cocky ass smile when she told him he'd gotten both her juices and her inspiration flowing. She pulled out her phone to drop him a line but remembered he would be in the middle of a practice session with his band. Not wanting to disturb him, she started calling Tasha instead but decided she would rather give her the *deets* face to face. She sent Tasha a text and asked her if she wanted to drop by the apartment to order pizza and catch up.

Tasha: Catch up? Mhmm. :). He turned that kitty cat out, didn't he? I can be there in a few hours.

CHAPTER EIGHTEEN

"One more time from the top?"

Cole loosened his grip on his bass guitar and glared at Xander. "No, Joe Jackson. I think we're good."

Xander turned to Jay for back up, but his friend eased from his keyboard and grinned. "You know your vocals are perfect. They always are. We don't need to do this set again. But if you are dead set that we do, I'm gonna need a break and something to drink."

He glanced to Cherry, a honey-hued sister who played the electric guitar and sometimes pitched in on vocals. Cherry tossed her bright red locs over her shoulders and scrunched up her nose. "I agree with Big C, Xan. Besides, Debbie and I are having a romantic night in tonight and I promised her I'd cook."

"I thought you said you loved this woman," Jay piped up. "Not if *you're* going to cook for her."

Cherry and Jay swiped back and forth for a while, earning laughter from Xander and Cole. Xander accepted that he was outnumbered. As much as he wanted to go over the set again, their band put everything to a vote.

"Anybody wanna grab a burger?" he asked instead. Cherry

declined, wanting to head to the supermarket to get a start on her dinner plans. Jay offered to go with her to give tips in return for a case of beer. They continued throwing jabs at each other, but Cherry agreed. Jay was actually a very good casual cook and Cherry... well... Jay hadn't told any lies when he asked why the hell she'd offer to cook for her girlfriend.

"I could be down," Cole said. "Wanna ride together?"

They packed up quickly before heading out to Cole's car parked out in front of his house.

Gary's Burgers had some of the best burgers Xander ever had. It was an unassuming diner, but there was nothing unassuming about their burgers. They ranged from the simple house burger, which, despite its simplicity, hit the spot every time to some crazy specialty burgers Xander couldn't find anywhere else. Whenever Xander suggested burgers, everybody knew the place wasn't up for debate. It was a good thing everybody he brought there was thoroughly converted.

"Hey Miss Rachel," he said greeting the owner with a hug. "How's it going?"

Gary, bless his soul, was her father and used to flip burgers in the joint when he was a teen and saved until he could buy it out from the then owners. Rachel took over after he died and Xander knew that wherever the old man was, he had to be proud of how she took things to the next level.

"Hey suga," she smiled. "You both gonna have your regulars?"

"Yes ma'am," Xander grinned. Rachel reminded him of his own mother in so many ways—from the soft, lilting cadence of her voice to her dark brown skin and dimpled cheeks. Navaya used to tease him that he came to the diner whenever he missed his mother. Remembering Navaya's teasing words brought other memories flooding back. He breathed deeply through his nose and exhaled slowly through his mouth, trying to center himself.

It didn't do him much good. He couldn't push out images of Navaya on her knees, back arched and taking him deep inside her. His dick twitched. Xander forced the thoughts from his mind and replaced them with something more benign. Music. He focused on the slow, jazz infused song that filled the restaurant, trying to place the voice. If he was paying attention to the music, he couldn't think about Navaya.

"You good?"

He flicked his gaze to Cole and tried to scrub his mind of thoughts of Navaya staring up at him with glassy eyes as she squeezed her breasts and moaned. If he lived to be a hundred, Xander was sure he would remember each cadence of Navaya's breathy mewls of pleasure. And he would get hard every time.

"Aye," Cole repeated. "Are you about to have a seizure?"

Xander sucked his teeth. "Whenever I think Jay got all the extraness in your gene pool, you remind me you can be a dramatic ass too."

He followed Cole to their usual table just as the waitress came by and took their drink orders. Cole settled for water and Xander got the sweet tea he couldn't get enough of.

"I saw your girl last night," Cole said.

Xander's brows pulled together. "My what?"

His friend ran a hand over his bald head as he chuckled. "Oh. Y'all didn't make up?"

Stefanie.

Damn. He hadn't thought about his short-lived relationship in a hot minute.

"Nah. There's no point."

Cole nodded. "There'll never be a point with Navaya around."

There were no teasing notes to Cole's voice. He was dead serious.

"You suggesting I ditch my best friend?"

Cole made a face. "Chill. I'm just saying that y'all are poison to the other's relationship. She'll realize that too once she puts herself out there again. And I can't necessarily say I don't see where the revolving door of women you try to date are coming from. Hell, I'm secure but I am not sure how secure I'd be with my girl describing her male best friend as her *non-sexual soul mate.*"

Cole's voice held the same incredulity it had when Xander first used those words to describe Navaya. He'd thought it was bullshit then. And he thought it was bullshit now. Xander's response died in his throat. *Non-sexual.* Those words didn't apply to him and Navaya anymore. He just wasn't sure that he wanted to let Cole in on that yet. Or at all.

He didn't have to.

"Fucking hell," Cole murmured.

"What?"

His friend paused when Rachel sauntered over with their fully loaded burgers and the waitress brought their drinks. He waited a full minute after both women left before he said, "You fucked Navaya."

"You have a hell of an imagination," Xander said, running his tongue across his suddenly dry lips. He chuckled. "Why would you think *that?*"

"You didn't see your face when I mentioned *non-sexual soulmates,*" Cole said before he screwed up his face in a consti-pated ass looking expression and burst out into raucous laugh-ter. "Yo... you looked like I caught you doing something *sickening.* So tell me... what happened? You got pissing drunk and face planted into her pussy."

He rolled his eyes. "That's crazy."

He and Navaya had been drunk, high, drunk *and* high around each other so many times and he'd never had any sexual thoughts about her. His friends always had a hard time believing him when he insisted he truly never thought of Navaya that way. That was why nothing made sense anymore. How did he go from never having sexual thoughts about his best friend to being unable to shut them off? He took a large bite of his burger so he didn't have to talk. How could he turn off sexual thoughts about Navaya now he knew the exact shape of her breasts? Now he knew how soft she felt against him. Now he knew how fucking sweet she tasted. How did he go back?

"So how did it happen then?" Cole asked. "Cause it did."

Xander considered whether he should tell Cole for a few seconds, but relented. Next to Navaya, Cole was his closest friend and although he and Navaya never kept anything from each other, he wasn't exactly sure how to bring up the confusion going on in his mind.

"She's been having a rough time with reviews over the last couple of months," he said, picking each word carefully. "She needed some inspiration."

Cole chuckled. "So she commissioned *your* dick. Nigga you should've gone with the drunk story."

His unexpected commentary caught Xander mid gulp of sweet tea and he almost snorted it all back through his nose. He grabbed some tissue and wiped his face. "Just cool. I'm sorry if the truth is too crazy for you."

"It *is* crazy. You both have gone on and on about there being no sexual interest between you. Why would she choose you instead of... well, literally anybody else?"

"You jealous, bruh?"

Cole shook his head. "Nah. Shorty is bad and all, but my attention is somewhere else. Firmly."

Xander raised an eyebrow. He hadn't heard Cole talk about a woman since his last situation ended on a sour note. "Oh really? When did you become *firmly* interested in someone?"

Cole laughed. "You're not going to change this conversation so don't even try."

Xander shrugged. "I'm all down for talking, but I'm going to need some *quid pro quo*."

Cole popped a fry into his mouth with a gruff laugh and shook his head. "Whatever, Donald Trump."

They ate in silence for a while before Cole eventually said, "You know I'm an open book but this situation is kind of complicated. It has the potential to be really messy."

"Messy?" Xander couldn't keep the disbelief out of his voice. Cole was probably one of the least problematic persons he'd ever come across.

"I'll tell you more when I can," he said. His voice was firm and left no room for negotiation. That only made Xander even more curious but he swallowed his questions.

"So..." Cole started. He let his voice fade off before he continued. "... was it weird?"

Xander thought about feigning ignorance but decided being stubborn wouldn't get him anywhere. He could use the advice.

"I expected it to be," he admitted. "Our first kiss was easily the most awkward kiss I've ever had. But then... I don't even know how to explain it. I've never had chemistry like that with anyone before."

Cole leaned back in his chair and observed him for a few seconds. "Shit. It's better than I imagined."

"What?"

His friend leaned forward, placed both forearms on the table and smiled. "So she ticks all your boxes. She's your *non-sexual soul mate* and now, apparently, the best sex you ever had. Just date her already and put all the poor souls to cross both y'all's path out of their future misery."

Just date her already. Xander would have laughed his ass off if Jay was the one sitting opposite him. But, Cole? He knew Cole was dead ass serious.

"That's insane," he said. "This is Navi-Nav."

Cole raised a thick, bushy eyebrow. "Why does the idea make you so pressed? You're one of the lucky ones. You've been telling anybody who would listen about how compatible you two are, how much she gets you, how much history you have... the only thing that seemed to be missing was sexual chemistry. Now, you're here telling me you've never had chemistry like that with anyone else. What exactly is your problem other than being God's favorite? Some of us are out here struggling on this boulevard of broken dreams."

"I'm not trying to fracture the most important relationship in my life because my curiosity got me more than I bargained for."

Cole's laughter irritated the fuck out of him. "You realize you'll never know another moment of peace in your life, right?"

The conversation wasn't going the way Xander expected it to go. And he knew the next words to come out Cole's mouth would piss him off. Still, he couldn't help but ask him what he was talking about.

"Let's say you fulfill this *mentordick* agreement or whatever your crazy ass arrangement is. She gets her writing inspiration, gets her groove back and then pops up with a nigga. How are you going to feel knowing he's going home to enjoy the best *you've* ever had?"

Xander tried to school his face into a neutral expression. He knew his unreasonable rage must have shown all over his face when Cole nodded his head and fixed him with a wry smile. "Yeah. I thought so."

CHAPTER NINETEEN

Well, damn.

Navaya scrolled down the Microsoft Word page filled with all the words she'd transcribed from her notebook as soon as she got home. She got in a good little editing session as typed the hastily written words. Navaya reread the scenes about three times and she felt a bit flustered. That was *the* best sign in her line of work. The scene which featured agonizing beats of delayed lust between her main characters was easily one of the best she'd ever written. She smiled widely as relief washed over her. She hadn't let on to anyone just how soul crushing it was to think she'd lost her spark. The anxiety was almost crippling when she worried she might never get that spark back. She pulled an unused notebook from the filing cabinet she kept fresh stationery in and sat down to flesh out the plot that formed in her mind when her phone rang. Navaya checked the caller ID before she answered.

"Hey, mama."

"How are you, lovebug?" Kathleen asked. "Me and Raquel are on our way to the farmers market and I thought I'd check in on my favorite daughter."

Navaya grinned. "You found yourself another daughter while I wasn't looking?"

"Perhaps," her mother teased. "How are you, dear? I see they haven't been kind to you on the Internet."

Navaya's cheeks went hot. She and her mother had a very clear boundary. Kathleen wasn't allowed to read anything she wrote. "Are you reading my stuff, mama?" she asked.

"No. A promise is a promise, but Xander told Raquel you were having a rough time."

Navaya made a mental note to strangle Xander before she answered her mother. "I was in a little rut but I think it might be behind me now."

"That's good. I was going to recommend that you went and got yourself a massage. Massages always do me good."

"I've been getting massages. Kind of," Navaya said, happy her mother couldn't see her smirk. Kathleen chattered for a few more minutes, passing the phone to Xander's mother whenever she thought Raquel might do a better job at explaining something.

"What's Xander up to?" her mother asked just as they started to wrap up the conversation.

"He's at rehearsal or something," Navaya said. "It might be easier to call him yourself. We're not joined at the hip."

Navaya expected her mother to comment about her sass, but Kathleen shocked her when she muttered. "Maybe you should be."

Raquel's giggle soon joined her mother's laughter and Navaya realized she was on speakerphone.

"Stop being messy," she heard Raquel say.

"It's about time them two make us related for real," her mother's muffled voice came through the phone. She obviously thought putting her hand over her mouth would be enough to prevent Navaya from hearing what she was saying. Navaya's mouth dropped open.

"What did you just say?"

There was more giggling from Raquel and her mother, but neither of them answered her question. Navaya rolled her eyes heavenwards. She knew she should just ignore the statement her mother never intended her to hear in the first place. Yet, Navaya couldn't let it drop. She wasn't sure if it was because of all the weird, conflicting thoughts she'd been having about Xander for the last couple hours, but she felt like she *had* to set their expectations straight.

"Xander and I are best friends. We're never getting together in that way. We'll never have those sort of feelings for each other."

Navaya recalled telling Callahan those near exact words when he'd gone into one of his usual insecure rants about Xander. Except, she'd been talking about sexual feelings then. And, well, the last few days taught her that she'd been very wrong. Could she be wrong about romantic feelings too?

"Xander's my best friend. That's it. We'll never be anything more."

"Okay, lovebug," her mother said in a soft subdued voice, clearly surprised with the tone Navaya had taken with her. She was sorry she'd hurt her mother's feelings, but she needed to warn her not to expect something that would never come about. Navaya sighed when she disconnected the call. She couldn't be sure if that warning was really meant for their mothers or for her own damn self.

CHAPTER TWENTY

Tasha's energy was off from the moment she stepped through the door. Navaya tried prying something, *anything*, out of her but Tasha kept brushing her off.

"We can just watch a movie and eat pizza," Navaya suggested. "I don't need to bore you with my drama."

She turned into the kitchen, fetched two wine glasses and was pouring wine when Tasha climbed on the bar stool. Tasha grinned at Navaya.

"Oh no," Tasha said. "I want to know *exactly* what happened with Xander."

Navaya's gaze lingered on Tasha's hand when she handed her the glass of wine and noticed her ring finger was bare of her engagement ring and wedding band. She remembered the weird comment her friend made about her marriage not lasting much longer and frowned.

"Tash?" she whispered. "Is everything okay with you and Jeremy?"

Tasha's forehead crinkled and her light brown eyes widened a bit before she fixed a questioning gaze on Navaya. She looked genuinely confused.

"Why would you ask that?"

Navaya took a small sip of her wine. "There was that comment at Starbucks and now you aren't wearing your ring. Plus, your energy has been... different."

"I was joking, Vaya. And the rings are getting cleaned."

The explanations were so reasonable that Navaya should have believed them, except she didn't miss the slight tightening of Tasha's jaw. She started to push, but the blaring doorbell pulled her up short. By the time she collected the pizza and returned to the kitchen, Navaya had time to accept pushing Tasha wouldn't help if something was wrong. And it would only annoy the hell out of Tasha if she was telling the truth that she was fine. Navaya decided it was best she dropped it... for now. Xander always told her that her biggest fault was never knowing when to leave well and good enough alone. She imagined his thick lips curving into a teasing smile if he knew she was finally listening to his advice. And then, suddenly, she was imagining those lips doing something else entirely. Her hands shook as she tried to put the pizza down on the island and she almost knocked her glass of wine over. Everything about her current situation was ridiculous and the more Navaya thought about it, the harder it was for her to stop the frustrated laughter bubbling in her chest from spilling out her mouth. Tasha watched her with a mixture of amusement and concern.

"And *I'm* the one with problems?" she laughed. "What the hell happened between here and the front door that turned you into a maniac."

Navaya massaged her temples and grimaced. "Let me start from the beginning."

"SO YOU JUST GONNA SIT THERE?"

Navaya and Tasha had moved from the kitchen with the entire bottle of wine and were sitting on the cushions on the living room floor. Navaya had gone through everything that happened between her and Xander, and Tasha was just sitting there staring with her mouth hanging open.

"Girl, you're going to have to give me some time to process!" Tasha said with a laugh. "I never pegged Xander as being freaky like that. This nigga made you come in a crowded ass restaurant. And... you let him? I'm speechless."

"You've said a whole damn mouthful for somebody who's supposed to be speechless," Navaya groused. Tasha rolled her eyes and popped a small piece of rolled up pizza into her mouth.

"No wonder you think you're confused about him," Tasha mused. "That's your pussy talking."

"Look," Tasha continued. "You're hot for him and that's a brand new feeling for you. Sometimes physical feelings are just that. The tenderness you are worried about was always there, boo. You were always ready to march into battle for that man. I've never seen anybody as protective or as in tune with another human being as you two. None of that is new."

Navaya turned Tasha's words over in her mind. Tasha made a whole heap of sense. Was she blowing everything out of proportion because it'd been so long since she'd been hot for anybody? She sipped her wine, grateful she chose to work out her feelings with Tasha instead of Xander like she'd been first inclined to do. That would have been embarrassing as hell when he probably came to the same conclusion that Tasha had.

"Welcome back to the game," Tasha said with a wide grin. "When this little thing between you and Xander wraps up, I don't expect you to be sending any of the men I fling your way back to me unfucked."

Navaya laughed even though what she felt wasn't amusement. She felt like Tasha had thrown a bucket of ice water into her face. It didn't matter what kind of man Tasha sent her way. Navaya wouldn't hold her breath that they could even begin to make her body feel the way Xander had. And if that wasn't trouble waiting to happen, Navaya didn't know what was.

CHAPTER TWENTY-ONE

Xander tried to keep his attention on the sausages he was browning in the frying pan while Navaya continued pouring orange juice into mason jars that were almost full to the brim with prosecco. There were three things in life that Navaya treated with utmost reverence: Her writing, her yoga and her mimosas. They'd been having brunch together on Sundays for so long now that Xander couldn't remember a time when they didn't. Sometimes brunch became a double date or a third-wheel sort of situation to appease whoever they were dating, but it was a tradition they both held on to. It was time to catch up on each other's week, as if they didn't speak all day every day, and shoot shit with each other. Xander couldn't think of one Sunday brunch where things were stilted or awkward between them. Except for today. Things were so awkward that Xander wasn't sure if he should confront it head on or hope things would level out. Just the fact he was censoring himself around Navaya was enough to aggravate the shit out of Xander. They did not censor themselves around each other. They were not awkward around each other. He swallowed a curse when he realized the sausage he was supposed to be paying attention to started to burn.

Navaya glanced over as she dropped the last of the fresh fruit into the mimosas. "I told you we should've gone for brunch at that new restaurant I suggested. They wouldn't have burned my food."

Xander was so grateful to see the teasing glint in her eyes that he almost suggested they headed to the restaurant she'd been dying to try for nearly a month.

"They wouldn't have served mimosas almost as big as your head, either."

She pulled her bottom lip through her teeth. "That was a good comeback. *Almost.* The glasses might be smaller but they have a bottomless mimosa option."

Xander struggled to keep his attention on the conversation at hand. "I'm never doing bottomless mimosas with you again, Navi-Nav."

He could tell from the way a smile lit up her face that she was having the same memory he was. The last time they went to a restaurant that boasted bottomless mimosas, they were both convinced the owner had been very close to kicking their asses out of his establishment. When Xander drove past the restaurant a few days later, he noticed a huge sign affixed to the front window explaining that their bottomless mimosa special now came with a limit to the number of mimosas each table could get before having to pay a surcharge.

The conversation picked up from there and soon Xander wondered if maybe he imagined the awkwardness because he was still tense from his conversation with Cole. They ate breakfast in comfortable silence and it was only when he cleared the table and Navaya returned to the kitchen to top up their mimosas that she turned to him with a megawatt smile.

"I was up until nearly three AM working on a new novella," she said. "I started after yoga yesterday and I think I might be nearly a quarter the way through."

An excited smile pushed the corner of his lips upwards. "Word? That's great, Nav."

She tossed a look at him over her shoulder as she topped up the prosecco and orange juice with a liberal pouring of vodka. "It is hot as hell too. I got no idea where it came from."

She dipped her eyes to avoid his gaze. He chuckled. They both knew exactly where it came from. Xander raised the mimosa Navaya handed him in a toast.

"Here's to the resurrection of the Queen of Smut."

Navaya giggled as she clinked her jar to his. "Thank you."

Xander raised his mimosa again and with a sly grin continued, "Here's to my dick; giver of inspiration, bestower of plots, conferrer of orgasms."

Navaya laughed until she gasped for air. "What the hell am I going to do with your corny ass?"

Xander's eyes dropped to her lips. He could think of a few things, but none of those applied now she'd gotten the inspiration she'd been seeking. He couldn't describe the disappointment that filled him. He hadn't gotten his fill of her. He wondered how she would react if he reached out and pulled her into him before kissing her until she lost her breath again. But he wouldn't try. He and Navaya's friendship was steeped in respect and he wouldn't fly in the face of that because he couldn't control the desire he shouldn't have in the first place. So, as much as he wanted to pull her into him so he could feel her curves against his body, Xander took a deep drink from his mimosa and said, "Just put some respect on my dick, Navi. Just a little respect."

CHAPTER TWENTY-TWO

Just put some respect on my dick, Navi.

Navaya's breath caught in her throat. She wanted to put a lot more than some respect on Xander's dick. But she couldn't help but notice that Xander wasn't trying to be about that life anymore. There had been one or two moments when the sexual energy between them was strong, but Xander was always quick to shut it down. *Open mouth; insert foot.* Why had she told him she got her groove back? She almost laughed at that. Of course she didn't think twice about telling him. Navaya was accustomed to sharing just about everything with Xander unless it breached someone else's confidence. She should have given some thought to the implications of telling him her creative juices were flowing again. They didn't have a reason to continue their arrangement anymore. She drank her mimosa so he couldn't see her frown. She wasn't ready for things to end. They'd barely gotten started. Her body heated when he turned to unpack his dishwasher and her eyes landed on his ass. A few nights ago she'd been digging her fingernails into his ass as she tried to pull him as deep inside her as he could physically get. She took another deep drink of the mimosa.

It was the vodka.

It had to be the vodka.

It was the only thing that could explain what she did next. Navaya took another gulp of mimosa and then spilled a good amount on her blouse. She watched the liquid seep into the light blue fabric and took a deep breath. She pulled the entire thing over her head before her commonsense kicked back in. Xander stared at her, eyes slightly widened, when he turned around and found her standing there about to undo the clasps of her mimosa soaked bra.

"Navi, what are you doing?" he asked. His voice was tight, and she didn't miss the way he grabbed on to the edge of the counter. She unhooked the bra and tossed it on the counter with her blouse.

"I had an accident," she lied. "I'm going to need to use your machine."

It took a few seconds for her request to sink in for how hard he was staring at her breasts.

"Sure," he said. "Let me get you a shirt."

His readiness to cover her up would have insulted Navaya if she hadn't believed it was coming from a place of self-preservation. When he stared at her breasts, and her hardened nipples, Xander looked... hungry. He wanted her. Navaya was sure. And she wasn't going to make running from it easy.

Her heart thudded hard against her chest, but she forced her lips into what she hoped was an easy smile. "Why? It's not like you haven't seen all of this before."

She gestured to her breasts, which brought his gaze right back to where she wanted it to be.

"Yeah but those circumstances were very different," Xander said. His voice just sounded pained now. She took a few steps towards him, hoping he wouldn't straight out reject her. Navaya wasn't sure her ego could withstand that.

"Were they?"

"Navaya," he said shaking his head a little as if he was trying to force out whatever thoughts he was having. "You wanted to see if you could get your inspiration back, and you did. We don't need to keep playing with fire."

"We don't *need* to," she said slowly. "But I think we both want to."

"Navaya..."

"We're both single. We're both grown. And... we both enjoyed each other. A lot."

She was close enough to him for her nipples to graze against his chest. His erection pressed against her. She raised her chin, caught his gaze and held it, willing him to make a move. They stood like that for a few seconds until Navaya started to take a few steps backwards. Xander grabbed her wrist and pulled her into him. His eyes were filled with something Navaya couldn't quite place, but she didn't have much time to think about it because his mouth crashed down on hers.

THIS WAS CRAZY.

They were crazy.

Xander couldn't find the resolve to stand firm in what he knew was the right decision. Not when she was standing half naked in front of him, daring him to accept what she was offering. He squeezed her waist and pulled her against the bulge in his pants, groaning when Navaya titled her head to the side so she could deepen the kiss. He plunged his tongue into her mouth and kissed her until they were both struggling to breathe.

"Are you sure?" he asked when he could finally pull away from her and put some meager distance between them. She nodded. That was all Xander needed to start yanking her yoga pants down. He sank to his knees and raised one of her legs over his shoulder as he pressed his lips to her sex. He exhaled roughly against her and held her still when she shivered. He hadn't imagined it. She really was the sweetest thing to ever coat his tongue. He pleasured her until her cries rang out in the apartment and when he couldn't stand not being in her anymore, he turned her to face to counter as he hastily pulled his joggers down. He pressed his palm into her lower back as he sank into her, closing his eyes tightly as the sensations overwhelmed his body. She arched her back as he found a rhythm. Xander grabbed onto her braids as he leaned down and planted a kiss against the center of her back. She screamed unintelligible things and then she screamed his name. Xander had to pause thrusting to stop himself from exploding right then.

"Fuck," he murmured.

He was in a whole heap of trouble.

CHAPTER TWENTY-THREE

It should have been scary how quickly they settled into a routine that included Xander in Navaya's bed more often than he was out of it. The last three weeks were a blur. Navaya knew it wasn't wise to get *too* accustomed to their routine, but it was hard. Xander showed up the night before with Chinese food and they sat on the floor of her living room eating directly from the takeout containers as Navaya worked on her manuscript and Xander worked on lesson plans. It was so damned comfortable and so damned normal that Navaya didn't think twice to lean her head on his shoulder while she proofread the words she put in. They'd finished their respective work and headed off to bed where they came together with so much tenderness that Navaya almost caught herself referring to it as *making love*. She'd pulled herself back into her lane with swiftness, but once she almost thought the thought, she couldn't seem to rein it back in.

Navaya pressed her ass into Xander and wriggled a little, knowing it would wake him right up. He wrapped his hand around her more tightly but didn't move. She shifted in bed so she could face him. He looked so peaceful with his lips settled into a stubborn pout that Navaya wanted to just let him sleep.

She couldn't though. If Xander wasn't up and out of her bed soon, he would be late for work. She wanted to bring up letting him keep a drawer of work clothes at her place but she was afraid he would read more into it than convenience, so she kept her mouth shut. As it stood, Xander hurried out of her bed way too early in the morning so he could get ready for work. She brushed her thumb across his cheek before leaning in to him and whispering in his ear. "I got front row seats to a John Legend concert."

His eyes jerked open. It took a few seconds before he became aware of his surroundings and the fact Navaya was messing with him. She did this at least twice per week and it worked every time.

Xander frowned. "You think it's funny?"

Navaya shook her head but she was having a tough time selling it considering she was laughing so hard her body shook. Xander tickled her until she begged him to stop.

He paused tickling her and held her gaze. She couldn't miss the desire in his eyes. "Have you learned your lesson?"

Heat pooled in her stomach as she shook her head and whispered. "No."

He brushed his lips softly across hers before he pulled back and smiled. "I need to use another tactic then."

XANDER RETREATED to the corner of the small dressing room the company the band was working with provided for them. It was an hour and a half to their call time and Xander couldn't remember the last time he'd ever been this nervous about anything. Navaya had just texted to tell him outside was packed. She wanted him to share in her excitement but knowing the biggest venue they'd ever booked was also full to capacity worked on Xander's nerves. The band had spent the last two years playing at bars and restaurants in front of less than a hundred people. They jumped at the opportunity to be one of the three local bands performing at the Kimani Showcase, a local fundraiser, knowing it would put them in front of more people than they'd ever been before. Their contact hadn't dropped the venue on them until six weeks before the show date, and Xander was floored when he realized it had a capacity of nearly six hundred people. Still, he hadn't expected the venue to be full. Xander's phone rang after a few of his dry ass responses.

"What's wrong?" Navaya asked as soon as he connected the call. The loud chatter behind her affirmed that the venue was indeed packed.

"Just nerves."

"You've got nothing to be nervous about," she said. "You guys are supremely talented. Especially you."

"Thanks for the vote of confidence," he said, feeling a little of the nerves dissipate. It wasn't nearly enough, though.

"It's not a vote of confidence, Xander," Navaya said. "It's a statement of fact. Try focusing on something else."

His laugh was humorless. "I don't think there's anything in the world that can distract me enough."

"Wanna bet?" she asked.

"If you have money to lose, sure."

She told him to give her a few minutes and then Navaya disconnected the call, leaving Xander wondering what the hell she had up her sleeve.

His phone dinged with a message about eight minutes later. He clicked on the attached photo and almost dropped the phone. Navaya had taken a topless photo in the bathroom and then edited the photo placing a 'G' and 'D' on either side of her breasts and 'Luck' under it. He burst out laughing so loud that Cole and Jay glanced in his direction. He didn't bother trying to explain anything to them. He glanced down at his phone when it dinged again.

Nav: I'll take my payment in crisp twenty-dollar bills.

CHAPTER TWENTY-FOUR

"Where did you disappear to?"

Tasha took a sip of her sugary iced drink and cast Navaya a suspicious glance. She'd barely given Tasha the heads up before she'd dashed out of her seat. Navaya considered lying. She wasn't ready to hear Tasha go another round of talking about how things were starting to seem *different* between her and Xander. Tasha had decided Navaya and Xander's feelings for each other had to be getting deeper and it didn't matter what Navaya said, she wouldn't shut up about it.

"What are you? The bathroom police?"

Tasha sucked her teeth. "You acting like I wasn't sitting right here while you were being supportive bae on the phone with your *beeessst* friend and then you upped and disappeared."

The extra three syllables Tasha put into the word 'best' had Navaya wanting to give her the cold shoulder for the rest of the night, but she couldn't. It wasn't Tasha's fault that her emotions were... tender... where Xander was concerned. Plus, she was happy to finally see Tasha returning to her normal self. She had been hot and cold over the last few weeks even though nothing Navaya tried could get the problem out of her. She'd gladly take the teasing in stride if it gave Tasha something to laugh about.

"He was nervous so..."

"... not you sitting there about to tell me y'all had a quickie in the dressing room."

Navaya laughed. Hard. "I've been gone for less than ten minutes, Tasha. What kinda sex are you and Jeremy having?"

"The kind where here masturbates into me." Tasha muttered and before Navaya could say anything she held her hand up and said. "I don't want to talk about it until I'm ready. I'm *not* going to talk about it until I'm ready. So don't waste the time that we can spend giggling about Xander to try to find out."

The anger in Tasha's voice caught Navaya off guard. A dozen questions flew to her lips but she clapped her mouth shut when Tasha squeezed her arm and said, "Please."

She nodded stiffly, hoping like hell that Tasha would eventually tell her what was going on so she could be there for her.

"I sent him a nude to distract him from his nerves."

She whipped out her phone and showed Tasha the edited photo. Her friend howled with laughter before she clapped her hand over her mouth to muffle the sound.

"Did you... did you use your boobs to spell out the word 'good'?" Tasha spluttered. "You're so damn chaotic."

Navaya smirked. "It worked."

"I bet it did," Tasha laughed. "Xander's nose is so wide open that I'm sure a picture of your little finger would have worked too."

"Tasha..."

Tasha gestured dismissively with her hand. "Yes, yes... I know, I know. It's just sex. Nothing happening there. He's your *beeessst* friend. I hear you. I just don't agree."

Navaya was saved from having to respond by the emcee announcing that the concert was about to begin. She sat back and listened to the first few bands to take the stage. Most of them had sets that comprised mainly or mostly of cover songs, but it didn't matter. Navaya always enjoyed the hell out of artist showcases. There was so much talent that often went undiscovered. Many people spent their entire lives rotating the same tired popular artists when there were so many more to explore. Navaya already scribbled down a band and two solo artists she planned to stalk online. Of course she might be biased, but none of those artists, as talented as they were, could hold a candle to Xander's band. Her favorite part of watching Xander perform was observing the people around her fall in love with his voice. That night was no exception. The band started off with a few covers before they rolled out their catalogue of original songs that had the woman sitting right next to her exclaim, "Who the hell are they? They bringing back the kind of R&B we deserve."

She wasn't lying. Xander commanded the stage like performing in front of hundreds of people came as naturally to him as breathing. Navaya would never have been able to tell he was a ball of nerves less than two hours before if she hadn't spoken to him. His smooth, deep vocals were as powerful as they were mesmerizing. She glanced around at the persons sitting closest to her. He completely captivated them. Pride blossomed in her chest. She wouldn't have been able to dim the bright, wide smile on her face if she wanted to as she listened to the rest of the set. She was on her feet screaming her head off as soon as Xander began announcing the end of the set. His voice was filled with more adrenaline than Navaya had ever heard before. She didn't care how odd she looked bouncing on the balls of her feet and screaming his name. Xander caught her eyes, winked and flashed her the widest smile and suddenly she was the one filled with nervous energy. She wanted to run up on the stage and throw herself in his arms while she told him how great he was, how proud she was of him and that everybody closest to her were just as impressed as she was.

Xander and his band absolutely killing their performance wasn't her accomplishment, but the happy excitement that filled her was making her head light. She couldn't imagine how excited Xander was and just thinking about that made her grin wider. Outside of her mother he was the most important person in her life. It was amazing seeing him take his first solid step towards making his dreams a reality.

"I guess you're going to screw his brains out to celebrate them bringing the house down, won't you?" Tasha teased once the applause finally died out and Navaya sat back down.

She laughed. "You bet your ass I am."

Tasha rolled her eyes. "Best friend, my ass."

CHAPTER TWENTY-FIVE

The energy in the dressing room once the band returned was electric. Even Jay had a hard time trying to find the words to express how he was feeling but it didn't matter. They could all relate. Xander went around the dressing room pulling his friends into hugs, not even bothering to get a handle on his amped up emotions. The thunderous applause still rang in his head making him feel like he was floating on air. Damn. The feeling was indescribable. Xander smiled when he thought about Navaya jumping in place while she screamed, smiled and clapped for him. He'd turned his head sharply to his left when he heard his name breaking up the monotony of applause. She waved a little when she noticed him noticing her and in those moments the crowd, the applause, the excitement faded away... nothing existed but he and the woman who rode hard as hell for him.

Mine.

The thought shocked him, but now he had a little time to reflect on it, Xander realized the panic he felt was an overreaction. He'd always considered Navaya to be his. It was in the way he always put her first, even when it put his relationships in jeopardy. He wouldn't have thought twice about the feeling if they weren't having sex. Cole had long stopped listening to him complain about not knowing what to make of the changing dynamics between him and Navaya. Cole thought the solution was simple: *try and see where things go.* It seemed so easy when he said it but Xander wouldn't fall into that trap. Everything was complicated as hell. Yet, in many ways they were still the same. He and Navaya still flowed easily together. She still knew him better than anyone else. She still made him laugh harder than anyone else. It was easy for him to just *be* around her. Their friendship dynamics hadn't changed in the slightest. But then there was the sex. A lot of sex. His body craved hers in a way he'd never craved anyone else's. When he kissed her, touched her, buried himself inside her and watched her screw up her pretty face as she came, things didn't feel friendly at all.

"Stop thinking about Navaya."

He pulled himself out of his thoughts and made a face at Cole. His friend chuckled.

"How do you know I was thinking about Nav?"

"Because you went from looking like a man who'd been granted all his wishes to a man with the world on his shoulders."

"You're doing the most right now."

Cole chuckled. "And you, my friend, are doing the least. I've never seen a nigga complicate an uncomplicated situation as thoroughly as you've been doing."

"It *is* a complicated situation."

"If you say so," Cole said with a shrug. "But all I'm saying is that the foundation for a great relationship is a solid friendship and you guys have that plus tax."

"I'm not trying to change me and Nav's relationship because I'm confused about my emotions."

"You mean the relationship you already done changed with your dick?" Cole shot back. "Anyway, I'm thinking we should grab the ladies and head out to have some celebratory drinks. Send your woman a text and tell her to gather up Tasha and Debbie and meet us out back."

YOU MEAN the relationship you already done changed with your dick.

Xander, Navaya, Cole, Tasha, Cherry, Debbie and Jay were on their second round of drinks at a bar down the road from the venue. Navaya insisted they did a round of champagne before they ordered their favorite cocktails. The joy on her face as she recounted how much the persons sitting next to her and Tasha enjoyed their set was enough to push Cole's comment to the back of his mind for a little while. Whenever there was a lull in the conversation or action, however, it came rushing back.

You mean the relationship you already done changed with your dick.

"You good?"

Navaya returned from the bar with a margarita and a whiskey sour. She handed Xander his drink and raised her eyebrow at him.

"Yeah. Why?"

She shrugged. "I don't know. Your energy seems a little off sometimes."

"I'm just tired," he lied. "I barely slept last night."

Navaya lowered her eyes and smiled when she raised them to find him grinning at her. His lack of sleep had nothing to do with nerves, but everything to do with the woman who scooted closer to him and raised her glass to his in a toast.

"You're about to be famous," she said. "I feel that in my gut."

"Does your gut have a timeline?" he teased. "It's been telling me I'm going to be famous for nearly seven years now but..."

She punched him playfully on his shoulder and he held her hand as she tried to pull it back, gently tugging her towards him. Her eyes widened for a few seconds as he brushed his lips to hers, but she accepted the kiss greedily. She grabbed on to the back of his neck and pressed her body into his as he stroked her tongue with his.

"Wait... what?"

Jay's confused exclamation had him chuckling against Navaya's lips before he slowly pulled away.

"I'm sorry," he whispered. "I got caught up."

"Don't sweat it," she responded with a shy smile as she brought her fingers to her lips.

"So... y'all a thing or something?"

"Mind your business, Jay."

Xander was grateful for Cole's interruption and figured after a few minutes the normal flow would resume around the table, but he was dead wrong. He didn't notice her until she was already standing right up in front of the table with her face twisted into an ugly scowl. Two of her friends hurried to her side and one held her hand, but Stefanie snatched it away.

"You fucking slut," she yelled at Navaya.

Navaya started moving towards the edge of the booth, but Xander grabbed her hand. "Don't."

To Stefanie he said, "Don't make an ass out of yourself, Stefanie."

"Shut up," she yelled. "You're a liar. Best friend? All this time I knew something was off and you kept gaslighting me. You made *me* feel like I was overreacting when you left my bed to run to hers at nearly one in the morning. I thought I had to be seeing things when I spotted you sticking your tongue down her throat."

"I never cheated on you."

Stefanie shook her head and laughed bitterly. "I hope you both rot in hell."

Her friends tugged on her arm again and this time Stefanie allowed them to pull her towards the exit.

Xander met Navaya's gaze for a few seconds to check that she was okay. She looked mortified but nodded at him to let him know that she'd be fine. The rest of the table didn't seem to know what to do with themselves. Debbie and Cherry studied the bar menu while Cole and Tasha whispered to each other. Jay's eyes roved from Navaya to Xander several times before he said, "Xander knew me and Quinn were in love with you, Navi."

He grinned widely as he took a sip of his rum and coke. "I'm disappointed as hell, but I can't say a nigga's surprised."

CHAPTER TWENTY-SIX

Navaya barely looked up from her computer when she heard her apartment door open. Her personal life was tethering towards chaos, but she'd never been as creatively inspired as she was now. Was her Muse living on the tip of Xander's dick? She chuckled before pausing and scribbling down a few lines just in case that stupid ass thought could become something interesting.

"I'm taking you for dinner."

Xander rubbed her shoulder as he leaned down and kissed her cheek. "How's the writing going?"

Navaya stretched before she pushed back her chair and stood. "I'm almost done. I should have it for you to review in a few days."

"Is anything going to seem... familiar?"

He gave her a lopsided grin that made her roll her eyes as she stepped into his arms. Navaya must have hugged Xander a billion times in their lives, but the hugs never made her feel like this before. She wanted to rest her head against his chest and stay there forever. When had she become so... needy? Things had been a bit touch and go since Stefanie's outburst at the bar the week before. Jay had diffused the situation by being his usual ridiculous self, but the awkwardness remained. It persisted long after she and Xander made their way back to his apartment where she made good on her promise to Tasha that she would screw his brains out. There were so many questions on the tip of her tongue but she couldn't bring herself to ask any of them. It wasn't the right time, she'd convinced herself, but she hadn't found the right time since. Navaya knew she was stalling. She had become used to whatever dynamic they had going on.

It'd been a month and a half since she recklessly suggested she and Xander added sex to their relationship and nothing about her life made sense since. If she were honest, she'd admit that this *thing* between them felt better than being with Callahan ever did. And that scared her. She and Xander needed to have a talk but tonight wasn't the night for it. Later, she promised herself. She couldn't put off this conversation forever. She excused herself to go get ready, grateful to put distance between them even though she almost gave in when Xander offered to shower with her.

She chose a green sweater dress, leggings and knee-high boots. She'd taken out her box braids two weeks before, so she pulled her natural curls into a high bun before swiping on a shade of lipstick she knew Xander was partial to. She sprayed two pumps of the subtle lavender and vanilla perfume he'd bought for her last birthday and then assessed her look in the mirror before deciding that she was satisfied with it. She returned to the living room to find Xander sitting in the darkened room just staring into nothing. Panic blossomed in her chest. She wanted to ask what was wrong but wasn't sure she was ready for the answer.

"Where are we headed?" she asked instead as she pulled a light coat from the closet in the hall.

"The Mussel Bar. I already made reservations."

The uneasy feeling returned in the pit of her stomach and Navaya suddenly knew what dinner would lead to. She took a deep breath and steadied herself, trying to ignore just how much it hurt.

You're crazy, her mind taunted, and she couldn't even deny it. He was her best friend. He knew all her dirty secrets. He'd had a front-row seat to all her embarrassing moments. She was insane for letting herself imagine this situation with Xander continuing.

"You ready?"

Navaya nodded, hoping none of her emotions showed on her face. If Xander was ready for things to go back to normal, she'd show him she was ready too.

⸻

XANDER WONDERED if Navaya could see how nervous he was. He kept sipping his water hoping it would soothe his suddenly dry throat but it didn't. He'd even brought her to the Mussel Bar. When he told Navaya he'd made reservations there, he didn't miss the skeptical look she shot his way. He didn't blame her. He had complained about how much he didn't enjoy eating there. Often. Eventually she got the point and came to the restaurant with Tasha instead. He figured it was a good strategy to ply her with her favorite wine and her favorite dishes before he asked her the question that might change the course of their relationship forever. Except, now that he was sitting opposite her watching her stir her cocktail, Xander wondered if he was making a mistake. The long ass talk he'd had with Cole the night before was still weighing heavily on his mind. Cole had come over with a six-pack of beers, got comfortable on Xander's couch and said, "I'm all ears."

He'd ordered wings, and they were halfway through eating before Xander finally took Cole up on his offer. He tried to articulate the confusing feelings he seemed to shift through a hundred times per hour.

"I don't get how you're *still* confused," Cole had said eventually. "I get in the start. It was weird and new, and more than a little crazy. But it has been weeks of you two doing relationship ass things with someone you already love."

Doing relationship ass things with someone you already love.

Cole had cocked his head to the side and waited for Xander's comeback. He didn't have one. He couldn't remember a night in recent times that he hadn't fallen asleep with Navaya in his arms or a morning he hadn't woken up to her gently trying to get him out of bed so he wasn't late for work. He usually got home from work, hit the gym and then was back to Navaya's place where they'd either go out to eat or order in food while she worked through plot points with him. In some ways things were just as they always were between them. Then she would say or do something and lust would punch him so hard in his gut that he couldn't breathe. In those moments he knew things were different as hell. But... was different bad? It sure as hell felt good when he fell asleep with her leg thrown across his body while he massaged the small of her back. It felt good as fuck when he slid into her and watched her make little faces that drove him wild. It felt good when he let himself into her apartment and she would stop whatever she was doing to greet him with a hug and a kiss. Cole was right. Xander and Navaya had fallen into a routine more natural and comfortable than half the relationships he'd been in. But would she think so too? Or would she find him presumptuous and laugh in his face? Navaya had been up front that it was sex she had been after.

"Ready to order?"

Navaya peeked up at him from behind the menu. "Is everything okay?"

We need to talk.

Except, he couldn't get the words out of his mouth. Instead he said, "Yeah. Just a little tired. Cole went extra hard on me at the gym today."

She grinned, bringing the dimple on the left side of her chin to the forefront. Xander licked his lips, his throat suddenly even drier. Damn. He knew Navaya was gorgeous. He wasn't blind and he had enough guy friends who were always talking slick shit about what they'd do if she was *their* best friend. He always shut down the conversation in ways that sometimes left his relationship with the offending dude fractured. He was protective as hell of Navaya, and he made sure everyone knew it. Xander couldn't work out how he'd gone so long without truly appreciating her beauty, though. It was crazy just thinking about how oblivious he'd been. How determined he was to not fall into the *fall for the best friend* stereotype. He'd argued with so many girlfriends repeatedly that women and men could just be good friends; that he and Navaya were really just *that* close.

"Why are you looking at me like you want to eat me?"

His lips curved into a slow smile. "Maybe I do."

Making Navaya blush was still a wonder to Xander. He was certain he'd never seen her blush before that night when he left her annoyed and aroused on her couch. Her eyes went all squinty and her lips quivered as she fought the smile that always eventually came. He wanted, as usual, to kiss that smile right off her face. Xander chuckled when he realized the only thing stopping him from doing just that was his own head. He eased out of the booth and slid in beside Navaya, cupped her chin and kissed her. She giggled into the kiss as her hands found the back of his head. She was still blushing when he pulled away and Xander decided he needed to put all his cards on the table.

"Navaya..."

"Excuse me."

Both Xander and Navaya glanced to the tall, dark-skinned woman with a short bob who was beaming at them.

"I hope this isn't too forward," she said with a soft giggle. "But y'all are beautiful together. Black love goals. Honey, you got yourself a cute one."

Xander glanced at Navaya expecting her to mirror his amused expression and was shocked to find her staring at the woman with horror on her face. His stomach sank. He got the answer to the question he'd been about to ask. Then Navaya made it worse.

"Nah, sis," she said with an awkward laugh. "This is my best friend. Shoot your shot if you want."

The woman glanced between them a few times as if she was trying to figure out who the fuck kissed their best friend like *that*. Eventually she apologized for her assumption and made her way back over to her table. Xander was grateful the woman brought her ass over to their table because she saved him from making a fool out of himself.

"That was crazy, wasn't it?" Navaya said with that same awkward laugh.

He took a sip of his beer and gave her a weak smile. "Yeah. Crazy."

CHAPTER TWENTY-SEVEN

Navaya tried to wash the discomfort she felt down with the freshly prepared cocktail the waitress placed in front of her. She still couldn't believe the woman wandered over to their table and fucked up the light flirtatious atmosphere that had started kicking off between them. She squeezed her eyes shut at the wave of embarrassment she felt when she recalled the interaction. Did she really have to tell the woman to shoot her shot at Xander if she wanted to? Navaya didn't miss the way his eyes flashed with irritation.

"I'm sorry," she said.

He raised an eyebrow. "For what?"

"That I pushed that woman on you," she replied with a small laugh. "She probably wasn't even your type."

She expected him to laugh along with her, but he didn't. He stared at her for a really long time before he finally said, "Nah. She was."

Navaya bristled with annoyance and then got angry with herself. She had no right to be in her feelings. She was still stewing in those feelings she wasn't supposed to have in the first place when he spoke again.

"You could've taken the compliment without all of that"

His tone pulled her up short. He sounded annoyed, *really* annoyed, and Navaya couldn't figure out why. His mood didn't improve even when the food came. Navaya kept trying to pull Xander into conversation but he rewarded her efforts with gruff, one-word answers until she gave up and just sat there and ate her food.

The minutes ticked by agonizingly slow. She was happy when Xander finally asked the waitress to pack up the food he'd been picking at. She remained quiet as he paid the bill and tipped the woman. It wasn't until they stepped out of the restaurant and on to the bustling pavement that she finally spoke. "We good?"

She pressed her tongue to the roof of her mouth and took a deep breath. Xander's body tensed slightly and he continued staring straight ahead. Navaya grabbed his arm and tugged, forcing him to bring his gaze to hers. She was so frustrated that tears starting pricking her eyes.

"Are we good?" she asked again. She could hear her heartbeat thundering in her ears as she waited for him to respond. *One. Two. Three. Four.* Five seconds passed before Xander turned to her and flashed her a wry smile. "Do you think we will keep ruining each other's relationships?"

Her steps faltered. She wasn't sure what she'd expected him to say, but it certainly wasn't *that*. She chewed on her bottom lip and acknowledged the disappointment she felt. A small part of her had hoped he'd been mad that she'd been quick to correct the woman about the true nature of their relationship. She'd *wanted* that. It would mean that perhaps he was feeling some of confusing emotions that plagued her.

"You think I ruin your relationships?" she asked hoping she kept some of the hurt that twisted her stomach into knots out of her voice.

He shrugged. "Everyone I've dated swear they see some version of whatever that woman saw. They'd grill me about whether we've been intimate with each other and they'd never believe me when I told them we hadn't. Then as soon as they figured the relationship was getting strong enough, they'd ask me to cut you off. It was always fifty-fifty if they'd stick around once I made it clear you'd always be in my life. Of course, even when they stuck around things eventually went the way it did with Stefanie."

Xander was always changing girlfriends and although every so often he'd tell Navaya they were insecure about their friendship, she hadn't realized he was asked to choose.

"You don't have to do that," she whispered. "You deserve an honest shot at a relationship."

"Even if it comes at the cost of our friendship?" he asked.

She swallowed what felt like broken glass lodged in her throat and lied. "Yes. At the end of the day I can't build a family with you and keep you warm at night."

But why not, her mind whined. Xander's entire face went blank as he came to a standstill in front of her apartment building.

"I'm going to head home," he said. He reached forward and pulled her into a hug—like he always did. Kissed the side of her head—like he always did. And promised he'd let her know when he got home—like he always did. Navaya struggled against tears as she watched his back retreat down the street.

Are we okay?

She wanted to scream it after him but it made no sense. Navaya already knew that for the first time in their entire friendship, she and Xander were definitely not okay.

CHAPTER TWENTY-EIGHT

"How did it go?"

Xander completed the last rep of his final set of overhead presses before he turned his attention to Cole, who'd been spotting him.

"It didn't," Xander said. Just thinking about his disastrous night with Navaya made his body tense.

"You didn't talk to her?"

Xander laughed bitterly. "Bruh. She isn't interested. At all."

He sighed at the open curiosity on Cole's face. Cole wasn't going to let it go until he got the details. Xander took a gulp of water, wiped the sweat from his forehead, took a deep breath and went into what was one of the most embarrassing nights of his life.

"She basically said I should put more effort into my relationships because I'll need someone to build with and that person wasn't her."

"Damn," Cole said. "That's not the read I got on the situation. At. All."

Xander shrugged. He pulled himself to his feet and started doing some stretches to soothe his aching muscles. He wished he had some stretches to soothe whatever it was that currently ached inside him. He wanted to call it ego... but Xander had a feeling it wasn't. He hadn't even felt this way when his last two relationships ended. He shook his head and laughed gruffly. Life sure as hell was full of surprises. Cole joined him on the mat to begin his own stretches.

"Something about that entire interaction seems off," he commented.

Xander chuckled. "Yeah... it was off because I let you convince me that Navaya might have been feeling me like that..."

Cole shook his head. "Nah, bruh. Don't drag me into that. I didn't convince you of anything."

Xander was about to fire off the smart ass remark on his tongue when Cole he raised a hand and double tapped his airpod and turned around. He didn't pay much attention to the call until he heard an edge creep into Cole's voice.

"Are you hurt?" he was saying. "Go straight to my place. I'll meet you there."

Cole's face was thunderous when he finally turned to Xander. "Yo, I'm going to have to go. Call Jay and Cherry for me. I gotta call off practice tonight."

"Is everything okay?"

Cole took a deep breath and grabbed his gym bag from the floor. "Make sure you pick up if I call you, 'kay? You might have to bail a nigga out of jail."

Cole stalked away before Xander could ask any questions. Cole was one of the most easygoing persons Xander knew, but he had violence written all over his face. He was almost sorry for whoever had made him so angry. He hoped it wouldn't really come down to him really having to bail Cole out of jail.

XANDER COULDN'T SETTLE DOWN. It didn't matter how many times he went through Netflix suggestions for the shows he should try out next or that his favorite podcaster had just dropped a new episode. He stalked to his fridge and stared at the empty contents for the fifth time before he accepted his restlessness was because he didn't want to be home. He wanted to be with Navaya. Xander couldn't remember a time when he thought twice about seeking Navaya's company out when he wanted it. But he was sure as hell second-guessing himself now. He grabbed another bottle of beer from the fridge, popped it open and headed back to the living room where he went through the Netflix suggestions... again. Xander chuckled as he thought of how much Cole would clown his ass if he knew he was pussyfooting around about heading to Navaya's apartment. Thoughts of Cole had him reaching for his phone. He was relieved to see there were no missed calls. Maybe he would end his night without having to go bail his friend out after all. It took nearly another hour before Xander stopped fighting himself. He grabbed his keys and called his and Navaya's favorite Chinese restaurant as he drove. He picked up the order of shrimp lo mien and sweet and sour chicken along with a cheap bottle of wine. He still felt a little raw from their dinner the other night, but Xander wasn't worried about popping up on Navaya unannounced. They'd work through any awkwardness they felt and Xander knew they'd be back to normal before they even finished the takeout. He was just about to cross the road to her apartment complex when he spotted her through the wide windows in the lobby. He slowed down, appreciating just how amazing she looked in ass hugging jeans, knee-high boots, a fitted red sweater and voluminous twist outs sitting on her head like a crown. He smiled, imagining burying his head in her hair and inhaling the scent of shea butter and peppermint that always clung to her strands. His smile faltered when a tall, dark man with his locs pulled back into a ponytail entered the lobby. Dressed in navy sweatpants and a white hoodie, he walked straight over to Navaya with a stride that suggested he'd come to meet her. Xander didn't recognize him, but Navaya's face broke out into a wide smile when she spotted him. She pulled him into a tight hug that lingered just long enough to make Xander's chest tighten. The man kissed her cheek before she touched his shoulder and pointed in the direction of the elevator bank. He watched them both disappear towards the elevator and stood there for a few minutes before he turned and left. His emotions raged. Was this why she was so eager to push him on another woman? He squeezed his steering wheel while he waited for the red light to turn green. Did it even matter? Navaya wasn't, and was never going to be, his woman. Before the last month, he'd never even entertained the thought of her being his woman. Except, her body fit like she was his. He knew her entire soul – dusty cobwebs and all. She felt like his. He didn't know how to go back to thinking about her in any other way. But he had to. He couldn't do life without Navaya. He glanced down at his phone when it began to buzz.

Nav: Hey. How did practice go?

Xander sighed. Their friendship was more important than any disappointment he was feeling. He would have to get things back to how they used to be before their ridiculous *mentordick* agreement; before he knew how she felt and how she tasted. But it wouldn't be tonight. He needed time to lick his wounds before he could pretend that Navaya didn't manage to unintentionally break his fucking heart.

CHAPTER TWENTY-NINE

The bar was dimly lit, giving off a faint blue glow. Navaya hadn't even known this place existed in DC but she liked the vibe. People were sitting around tables and in loveseats pushed up against walls decorated with large black and white photos of musical instruments. Navaya approached the bar and ordered herself a glass of wine. She dug through her bag for her phone and pulled up her chat box with Xander. The message she'd sent him the night before remained unread. A sharp zing of anger shot through her, but she took a deep breath and allowed it to seep out. She almost didn't come to Xander's gig, but she'd never missed one of them and she would not start even though she was pissed at him. The bartender handed Navaya one of the largest glasses of Cabernet Sauvignon she'd ever seen. Another point for the bar. She handed him her card, but he brushed her off.

"It's on me," he said with a wink.

She smiled and thanked him. She'd put in a hell lot of effort into her appearance. She wore a form fitting backless burgundy dress that stopped just above her knees with ankle boots. She was grateful that the weather wasn't too bad yet, so she didn't freeze her ass off on her way to the bar. She pushed strands of her freshly pressed hair behind her ear and took a deep sip of her wine before turning her attention back to her phone. Xander wasn't the only friend acting weird. Tasha had been responding to her messages erratically and with one-word answers for the better part of two days and refused to answer her calls.

Navaya: You got to talk to me, Tasha. I'm dead worried about you.

Tasha: I will. I just need some time. How about we meet up next week?

Navaya: Deal. I'll come around to yours with a bottle of wine.

Tasha: I'm not really at home right now. I'll meet you at your apartment and we'll talk about it then.

Navaya: Where are you?

Tasha kept typing and deleting her message before she finally responded by telling her she was with a friend. The response didn't really do much to soothe Navaya's worry.

Navaya: Are you okay?

Tasha: Yeah. I promise. I'm safe. See you next week.

Navaya sighed. *I'm safe.* Her heart thudded against her chest as she took in that line. Was Tasha saying that at some point in time she wasn't? She dialed Tasha's number and wasn't surprised when she didn't pick up. She made her way to the quietest corner of the bar and called a few more times. She'd just about given up when the call finally connected.

"Hey, Nav."

The phone almost slipped from Navaya's fingers. "Cole?"

"Tee's fine," he continued. "I know you're worried but the calls are overwhelming her right now. She'll talk to you."

Navaya tried to make sense of everything but kept coming up short. What the actual fuck was happening?

"You answering Tasha's phone calling her by a pet name when I didn't even know y'all talk like that isn't helping, Cole."

"You trust me?"

She scoffed. "I do but..."

"Then trust me," he said. "And please don't tell Xander anything about this."

Xander's name brought her back to her surroundings. She glanced towards the stage in the middle of the bar where Xander, Cherry and Jay had set up.

"Wait. You're not coming tonight?"

"Cherry got me covered," Cole said softly. "I needed to stay with Tee. Tell me how much they suck without me, 'kay?"

He hung up before she could say anything. She tried to shake away the unease and confusion she felt as she made her way nearer to the stage. Xander caught her eye as she placed her glass of wine on the side table next to the nearest couch. She waved at him and he waved back. Navaya frowned. Was she just imagining how unenthusiastic that wave was? She'd intended to go over and say hi, but Navaya picked up her wine and settled into the couch instead. She was scrolling through social media, tapping her foot and singing along to Ari Lennox talking about someone breaking her off and doing it how she liked it when she spotted movement out of the corner of her eye. She looked up in time to see a short, curvy woman with the deepest brown skin, dressed causally in jeans and a slouchy top approach the band. Xander smiled widely when he saw her. He hugged her before he went back to adjusting the mic stand while they continued chatting. She laughed at something and Navaya couldn't untwist the anger that knotted inside her. Who the hell was she? And why was he being friendlier to this woman than he was being to her?

Just leave.

She wanted to, but morbid curiosity kept her ass glued to the couch. Her confusion deepened when she realized Xander had saved a seat right up front for this unknown woman. Navaya watched as she sat down and crossed one slender leg over the other and ran her hand through her short curls. Xander kept stealing glances at her throughout the entire first half of the set and by the time intermission rolled around, Navaya thought she'd explode with anger. She slinked off the bar just as he settled in beside the woman on the couch, but she called off the order before the bartender could hand her the wine. She wasn't interested in staying anymore. Xander surely didn't need her support. He seemed to have plenty from whoever that was whose face he couldn't seem to get out of.

You told him to go find someone to build with.

Navaya took a deep breath, trying to ward off the angry tears that pricked her eyes. She turned and walked right into Xander's chest. She was angry and frustrated as hell, but her body still flushed when she felt the warmth of his hand against her arm.

"I was looking for you," he said.

"Sure," she chuckled, not caring how much attitude was in her voice.

Xander's eyes widened. "You good?"

"I'm just leaving."

Creases formed on his forehead as his confusion seemed to deepen. "We're only halfway through."

"I think you'll be just fine without me," Navaya shot back. She cringed at how petty and juvenile that sounded, but she was beyond caring. Xander grabbed her hand as she started walking away. She yanked it away from him. Hard. A few persons milling around looked on at them and she didn't miss the horrified look on Xander's face before she turned away and started moving towards the door. Shame and embarrassment filled her, but it was nothing compared to the aching pain in the middle of her chest that seemed to widen with each step she took.

"What have I done?" she whispered.

CHAPTER THIRTY

Navaya held it together for the journey home. She didn't think anyone would enjoy listening to her sob her ass off on the Red Line back into Maryland. She finally let her emotions take over now she was wrapped up on her couch with a glass of brandy. She couldn't even keep track of the fatalistic thoughts running through her mind. She shot back the brandy in one gulp before pulling out her phone. She needed to get out of her head. She needed someone to tell her that the doom and gloom scenarios she was painting in her head were unrealistic. She'd get over her silly little crush. Her body wouldn't always remember the feel of Xander's fingertips trailing down her spine quite as vividly as it did now. Eventually she would be able to sit across from him and the woman he would build with and smile while being genuinely happy for them. She squeezed her eyes shut against the pain she felt when her mind conjured up that image. Eventually, but not tonight. What she couldn't handle was losing him as a friend. He'd been such an essential part of her life... for her entire life, that she couldn't even begin to understand how she would move through life without him. Navaya was nursing her third glass of brandy when she heard the key turn in her front door. She was disoriented for a few seconds before dread filled her. She wasn't anywhere near ready to face Xander right now. He stood in the archway of the living room for a full minute while Navaya struggled to breathe before he said anything.

"Look," he said. "It's time to sort out whatever the hell is going on. I don't like being at odds with you. There's no reason for me to be at odds with you."

"You didn't seem to care too much about being at odds with me while you were ignoring me tonight."

Xander narrowed his eyes. "You yanked your arm away from me and ran from the bar when I tried to catch up with you at intermission. What are you even going on about?"

Anger propelled her off the couch. "You spent the entire night all up in some woman's face. You barely acknowledged my presence."

"Since when have you been needy for my attention?"

She stepped back as a fresh wave of anger washed over her. "*Needy?* You have fucking nerve. I'm sorry I figured I deserved more than a half dead wave after I trekked down to DC to hear you play the same set for the thousandth time when I could've been doing so many other things."

"I don't force you to come to my gigs," he said in a soft, angry voice that riled her up even more. "Fuck you, Navaya."

"I wish you never did," she screamed shocking the hell out of herself, and out of Xander too from the way his body went stiff.

His face twisted into something ugly when he said, "Sorry your replacement dick came in a few weeks too late."

That knocked the wind out of Navaya. "Replacement dick?"

Xander fixed a hard stare on her. "I saw you in you lobby

yesterday, Navaya. I was trying to make sure Annalisa was comfortable since she is our potential manager for fuck's sake. I can't believe you are really here going off on me when I watched you hang off a nigga before you brought him back up here."

"Kasey's a friend from yoga and came by so I could help him write poem for his wife's birthday. You could've just asked me instead of jumping to conclusions like an ass."

Xander leaned against the wall and raised an eyebrow. His words came rushing back to her and Navaya wished the ground would swallow her up.

Potential manager.

Her anger deflated like a balloon.

"I was just..." she tried to find the words to explain the over-whelming emotions she felt the longer she watched him interact with Annalisa.

"Jealous," he supplied. She wanted to argue, but she didn't have any fight left. He was right. She'd been jealous as hell. Xander started speaking before she could say anything else.

"I was jealous yesterday. I didn't know who the fuck he was but I wanted to drag him off you."

He'd moved close enough to her that their bodies touched. Navaya swallowed hard. "Why?"

She hated the way her voice came out all breathless and shaky.

"Because," Xander said slowly. "I imagined him doing this..."

He brushed her cheek with his thumb and dragged it down to her lips.

"And this..."

Xander circled her waist and pulled her into him. Navaya's throat went dry.

"And this," he whispered before lowering his head and

brushing his lips against hers. Her body flared immediately. She sighed into the kiss before her mind kicked in and she pressed her hands to his chest as she backed away.

"We shouldn't..."

"Why not?"

"We shouldn't have crossed that line," she said. She closed her eyes, knowing it was the second lie she'd told in as many minutes. She didn't regret having sex with him, but she regretted the fall out. She regretted the confusing emotions she felt. She regretted wanting more, even though she knew she couldn't have it.

"Do you seriously believe that?" he asked. He'd taken a step back but was still close enough that she could see the creases formed at the corner of his eyes. Close enough that their bodies would touch if she leaned forward an inch. His voice was filled with incredulity and a bit of hurt. Navaya shook away the small flutters in her chest. She had no business hoping for anything. Look how great that turned out the last time.

"I'm confused," she said after a few seconds. "What do you want me to say?"

"That you feel all the things I've been struggling with for the past couple weeks," he said.

She brought her gaze to his. There were so many emotions in his eyes. She swallowed her discomfort at the vulnerability she saw there. Hope soared high in her chest, but she pushed it back. She still felt so fragile and she was afraid the disappointment would break her if she was reading too much into his statement.

"What have you been struggling with?" she asked softly. She wanted to look away as she waited for the answer with anticipation unfurling wildly in her stomach, but she couldn't. She didn't miss the way his lips quivered as he ran his tongue across them before he took a deep breath and spoke again.

"I've loved you for my entire life," he whispered. He paused for a few beats like he was working up the courage for the words to come. Navaya couldn't breathe. "But now I'm falling in love with you."

CHAPTER THIRTY-ONE

Xander felt lighter now he finally got the words out. Navaya just stood there, still as hell, with her eyes widened in shock.

"Are you... are you serious?"

He nodded. "Uncomfortably so."

She stared at him for what seemed like forever before a wide smile spread across her face. "I thought I was falling alone."

I thought I was falling alone.

The last few boulders sitting on his chest shifted and Xander felt like he could breathe again. He reached forward and cupped her cheek. "Nope, Navi-Nav. You're not alone."

She accepted his lips when he bent his head, sighing into the kiss as his hands went to her waist. She pulled back way too soon for Xander's liking and when she looked at him again, worry filled her eyes. "What do we do?"

He hadn't expected that question. Hadn't he made it obvious that she was what he wanted? "What do you mean?"

"Feelings are one thing, Xan," she said. "But... there is so much at stake here. What if we fuck this up and I lose you?" Her voice quietened and shook a little as she continued, "I don't want to lose you."

He cupped each of her cheeks in the palm of his hands as he brought his forehead to hers. "You *can't* lose me."

"Look at what just happened. We've never argued like that before."

He chuckled. "We've never had these kinds of feelings before, either."

The worry in her eyes remained and so he placed a quick kiss on her nose. She scrunched up her nose but smiled. His heart beat hard against his chest as he spoke again. "You know what I realized while you were trying to tell me to ditch our friendship the next time a woman asked me to choose? I will always choose you. Every time. Without hesitation. No matter what's at stake."

"Xander..."

"I can't promise things will always be great. I can't even promise you that this will work, but I know that we could never truly lose each other. It doesn't matter how long or how much work we'd have to put in to find our way back to where we started... we would get there. We're stuck with each other."

She smiled then, and it was like sunshine. "This is all so..."

"Weird?" he finished.

They laughed together when Navaya said, "Look at us becoming one big stereotype and falling for each other."

"I'm not going to lie," Xander confessed. "This makes me anxious as hell, but I can't imagine not trying."

Navaya tilted her chin upward and kissed him. It was soft, sweet and filled with the promise of more to come. Her grin was wicked when she pulled away. "You're going to have to be the one to tell our mothers."

XANDER WAS SPRAWLED out on the bed with the sheet riding low on his thighs. He mightn't be awake, but his dick was. Navaya chuckled. They'd made love the entire night with the moonlight filtering in through her bedroom window. It felt so good to finally be able to express the tenderness she'd been feeling through each touch and kiss. She'd expected to be sated, but sunlight was barely filtering into the bedroom and her body craved his again. She straddled him and leaned forward, planting a kiss on his forehead. She kissed his lips before sliding down his chin and neck to his Adam's apple. His hands came to her waist and gripped her. She raised her head and smiled at him.

"Good morning, Xander."

He grinned widely and her stomach did flip-flops. "Good morning, girlfriend."

Damn him for knowing how to make her feel so incredibly soft. She welcomed the sweet pressure of his lips against hers as she lost herself in the kiss. She could kiss Xander forever, but the lust in her belly demanded more. She continued her trail of kisses down his chest to the top of his thigh as she wrapped her hands around his erect dick. She smiled at his sharp intake of breath when she began stroking him slowly. Navaya tightened her grip and quickened her strokes before she replaced her hand with her mouth, relishing the way he felt against his tongue while she took him to the hilt. She hummed as she slid her mouth back up his shaft and took him in again. Xander fisted his hand in her hair as he raised his hips slowly to meet her and then quicker still until she had to wrap her hand in the sheets to keep steady. She'd thought she couldn't get wetter, but her body proved her wrong as she relaxed her throat to take as much of him as she could as he continued thrusting into her mouth.

"Damn Nav," he murmured. She loved to hear the strain in his voice, knowing how close he probably was to coming undone. She took him in one more time before she licked her way up his dick, placing a dainty kiss on its head. She grinned as she wiped away the excess saliva around her mouth with the back of her hand so she could lean forward and kiss him. His tender exploration of her mouth surprised her considering she could feel the head of his dick pressed up against her entrance. She sighed into his mouth when he finally slid inside. Navaya didn't think she would ever tire of this, not when their bodies moved like they were made for each other. She buried her head in the crook of his neck as she rode him, driving herself closer and closer to the edge. She came with his name on her lips and after a few more languid thrusts, Xander came along with her. He kissed the side of her head as she settled on his chest.

"I'd really thought sex with you couldn't get any better," he said with the most adorably dazed smile on his face.

Navaya chuckled. "Has it?"

"Definitely."

She eased herself up off his chest so she could look at him. "Really? What's changed?"

Xander tipped her chin upward before dropping a quick kiss on her lips. When his eyes met hers, Navaya almost melted at the love she saw there. "Now you're mine."

EPILOGUE

Happy. Grateful. Blessed.

The last ten months of her life had been filled with so many professional and personal blessings that Navaya often wanted to pinch herself to make sure she wasn't dreaming. Her latest release had been sitting at the top of the bestsellers list for the third week running. And then there was Xander. There wasn't a day Navaya didn't wake up with her heart full and pussy drenched from the amazing man she couldn't wait to spend the rest of her life with.

"You need any help?"

Navaya pulled her attention away from the mimosas she'd been fixing to stare at Xander. She shook her head but rolled to the balls of her feet and kissed him.

"I'm good, babe. You can go control our mothers before they tell everybody more embarrassing stories."

He chuckled and then wandered off to the living room where Navaya could hear raucous laughter from Tasha. She shook her head and smiled, wondering what Kathleen or Raquel had just shared. As Navaya poured the orange juice into the mason jars, the diamond engagement ring she'd yet to get accustomed to wearing glittered in the sunlight. She smiled widely. It seemed like everyone knew Xander had been planning to propose except her. Their mothers showing up unannounced two days before should've been the first clue, but Navaya had accepted their excuse that they had flown down to watch Xander's gig. The band released their first EP independently a few months before and it was doing so well they had a meeting lined up with a record label. She'd been excited for their mothers to see how amazing Xander was at performing and was enjoying the hell out of the gig when he suddenly announced he had a song he wanted to debut. She'd been surprised because Xander never mentioned working on anything new, but soon she was busy trying to stop herself from flooding the floor with tears and her heart from erupting in her chest. *Always Right There* was a soulful ballad about finding true love with someone who'd been right under his nose all along and Navaya had already been crying because she thought it was beautiful. She was confused when Xander started coming down from the stage towards her and had barely started putting things together before he was down on one knee.

"Navaya you've been my best friend my entire life, my soul mate as soon as I knew what unconditional love was and my lover for the most amazing ten months. I don't ever want to do life without you by my side. Will you please, please, *pleeaaase* agree to be my wife."

It had taken a full two minutes before Navaya could stop crying long enough to answer the question and she barely registered when he slid the pear-shaped diamond ring on her finger. All she'd cared about was being able to bring her lips to his and wrap herself up in his arms even as the audience's cheers and their mothers' excited chatter faded into the background.

"You reliving the proposal again?"

Navaya grinned at Tasha leaning up against the fridge chuckling at her.

"Perhaps."

Tasha grabbed a mimosa and took a small sip. "I hope you made some less potent ones for your mothers because I don't think we could handle them drunk."

Tasha laughed at her own joke, and Navaya's heart swelled. Tasha had the roughest couple months and Navaya was happy to see some light finally return to her eyes.

"How are you doing?" she asked.

"I'm good, Nav. You don't have to ask every hour."

"I know but..."

"You had to invite Cole," she said. "He's Xander's newly promoted best friend and likely best man. I got it. We can be civil to each other. It's okay. I know it's your party but come help me set the table."

She and Tasha worked together to set the table for the brunch styled engagement party Tasha and Xander planned. They left the mimosas up to her because they knew how seriously she took them.

Brunch was a whirlwind of laughter, funny stories and people telling them that this was bound to happen. People giggled every time they saw her casting a sideways look in Xander's direction, assuming she was in the throes of love. Navaya chuckled. The only thing she'd been in the throes of throughout brunch was an orgasm. Xander alternated between leaving the Lovense Lush on a pre-programmed setting and making patterns with his finger that had her squirming in her seat. Navaya took deep breaths, very aware that her mother was watching her with the eyes of a hawk.

"Are you okay, lovebug?" her mother asked. "You look peaky."

Her mother glanced at Raquel and Navaya shook her head when she saw the small smile on both of their faces.

She started speaking but stopped when Xander increased the power of the vibration. When she finally got her breath back, she turned to her mother. "I'm not pregnant, ma. Stop getting excited."

Everyone around the table chuckled and she used their distraction to excuse herself to the bathroom. She wasn't surprised when Xander followed her.

"I can't believe I let you talk me into this," she said.

He chuckled. "I didn't talk you into anything. You love when we do this."

She smiled because he was right. She and Xander would take the vibrator along to dinner a couple times per month. The aim was always to bring her as close to an orgasm as possible but never allowing her to actually get off. The sex afterwards was always scarily intense.

"I don't think I'm going to last the entire brunch," she said.

"Let me help you out."

He set the vibrator to one of the steadiest settings before he kneeled in front of her and lifted her dress above her hips. Navaya swallowed a scream when he flicked his tongue against her clit. He grabbed on to her thighs as he lavished her pussy while the vibrator persistently throbbed inside her. She bit her lip, arching her hips and pulling him into her. Navaya would never get used to how much Xander worshipped her pussy. She grabbed on to his shoulders to steady herself as the pleasure continued to build. Her body felt like it would turn in on itself when the orgasm finally washed over her. Navaya still shook even as Xander pulled her dress back down and rose to his feet and kissed her greedily.

"You see how sweet you taste?" he murmured against her

lips. "Come on, Diabetes. Let's go entertain these people so they can go. I've got a tree I think my fiancée would love to climb."

###THE END###

AFTERWORD

Navaya and Xander were a pleasure to write. I hope you love them as much as I do.

If you liked this book, please think about rating it and/or leaving a review on Amazon and/or Goodreads and telling your friends about it. Word of mouth is so important for indie authors.

Peace. Love. Light.
Rilzy

ABOUT THE AUTHOR

Rilzy Adams believes all you need is love. Or, at least it should. She may, or may not, be a huge Beatles fan. She spends too much time living in her head watching the romantic lives of her 'imaginary friends' play out and then being the chatty friend to tell the world about them. When she isn't living in her head, she must show up to work every day and be a lawyer. She resides, with her two dogs, on an island in the middle of the Caribbean Sea, which is perfect for her sun addiction, love affair with Prosecco and sushi worship.

For information on new releases, promotions and more: Join the Mailing List.

Visit her website at: www.rilzywrites.com

ALSO BY RILZY ADAMS

FALLING LIKE A JOHNSON SERIES

The Gift (Jaxon and Maya)

Will You Be Mine? (JT and Hallie)

Just One More Time (Orlando and Katrina)

When Love Ignites (Jasmine and Alec)

The Sweetest Escape (Jasper and Reign)

Yours Always (Orlando and Katrina)

LOVE ON THE ROCK SERIES

Twelve Dates of Christmas (Zia and Rashad)

You, Me + Baby (Fran and Andre)

Brand New (Regina and Quentin)

SINGLES

Off Key (Zoe and Liam)

Love in the Time of Corona (Alyssa and Kingsley)

SHORT STORY COMPILATIONS

Love Bites – A Collection of Short Stories

Printed in Great Britain
by Amazon

67474578R00083

It was all supposed to be so simple.

Navaya Howard is an erotic writer in a rut. Her readers are fed u
her stale plots and Navaya can't blame them. She's been celib
for over a year and a half since finding her now ex-boyfriend's
chick's positive pregnancy test on her bathroom counter. How
she write steamy romances if she can barely remember which b
parts go into the other?

Navaya enlists the help of her best friend, Xander, to revive
inspiration that used to have her sitting comfortably at the to
her game. What happens when the sex hits deeper than eithe
them expected and the tender emotions can no longer be den

Navaya and Xander's arrangement has gone far deeper
intended.

Will their friendship and their hearts survive the fall?

ISBN 9798670273657